THE DETERMINED AMISH BACHELOR

SEVEN AMISH BACHELORS BOOK 6

SAMANTHA PRICE

AMISH ROMANCE

CHAPTER 1

TIMOTHY HAD DRAGGED himself out of bed, and he stood warming his hands around a large mug of coffee as he looked around the depressing apartment. His two housemates had moved out, leaving him to pay the rent. Of course, he could have gotten other people in to take their places but he was too afraid of landing young men who led an outrageous party-going lifestyle. He had done enough of that, and now he wanted to lead a quiet life and persuade Taylor to marry him.

His cluttered apartment sorely needed spring cleaning, and the mess was only serving to push him further into a state of depression. He pushed his hand through his hair and was reminded that it needed a good trim. Living by himself was something he'd grown to detest. If all went well, Taylor would marry him, and when she had the baby, they would all be a happy family. That was his dream, and now he just had to make that happen. He swallowed a mouthful of coffee just as the doorbell rang.

With a sigh, he placed the coffee mug down on the table and headed to the door, glad that he was at least dressed and ready to face the day and his unexpected visitor. When he opened the door, he was surprised to see his newest sister-in-law standing there.

"Mary Lou! This sure is a surprise." He wedged himself in the doorway so she couldn't see into the dirty apartment.

"You've been on my mind lately, and since it was such a lovely day for a Saturday, I stopped by to see if there was anything you needed help with."

He frowned. "Shouldn't you be off with my *bruder* doing things that newlyweds do?"

Mary Lou chuckled. "He's busy doing something today. We don't need to live in each other's pockets you know, just to prove to people that we're in love. We are very much in love."

Timothy raised his eyebrows. "Err, I didn't say that you weren't."

"I know that some think we're an odd match,

but that's just the way things worked out. Jacob loves me, and I love him right back." She moved forward, trying to make her way into the apartment.

"Good. I'm glad we cleared that up." He moved to block her way.

"You don't want me to come in?"

"I'd rather you didn't."

"Why not?"

He looked down, embarrassed to admit the mess that had come about from neglect. If Mary Lou told his mother how dirty his apartment was, that would give *Mamm* another reason to be upset with him. "It's not for visitors."

"Oh, that's all right. I'm used to how messy boys can be. Jacob was a bit messy until I trained him. I can help you clean up if you like. I have all day."

"Really? You'd really help me clean?"

"Of course. What's a *schweschder*-in-law for if I can't help out every now and again?" He stepped back and opened the door widely. She looked around and took a tentative step forward. "Oh, my. You didn't exaggerate."

He rubbed a hand through his hair. "Everything's a mess, and I feel bad about it, but I just can't face doing anything at the moment."

"I'll do it, and you can help. It won't take us long at all."

"How do you figure that?" He looked around; empty pizza boxes sprawled on the coffee table, his clothes and shoes were strewn on the floor in the living room, and nearly every dish and plate in the place had been used and not washed.

"If we get going and work hard we'll have this done in no time at all."

"*Denke,* Mary Lou, I appreciate this."

"I just finished cleaning my *haus* this morning. What you need to do is do a little bit every day, and then it doesn't add up until you're faced with a … a …"

"Something that looks like a tornado hit?"

"Exactly."

"It's hard with the hours I work. I do two jobs and am so tired when I get home. I used to clean, but then everything just got dirty again, so I figured it was a waste of time."

Mary Lou put her hand over her mouth and giggled. "It's the same as eating. You don't say, 'I ate last week,' or, 'I ate yesterday and I don't need to eat again,' do you?"

"I guess not."

"That's like cleaning. It needs to be done every

day if you want to stay on top of it."

"I see. I'll try to do that, I really will."

She picked up three of the pizza boxes and looked around. "Where's your trashcan?"

"It's full."

"Well, find somewhere to empty it and bring it back to me. Then we can throw out all the rubbish. That's the first thing we'll have to do."

Timothy took the three pizza boxes and the full trashcan out to the dumpster where all the other apartment dwellers dumped their trash. He was pleased Mary Lou cared enough to visit and see how he was. His mother and father just viewed him as a disappointment lately, but Mary Lou wasn't judging him. She was more like a big sister than a sister-in-law. He'd known her for many years, since she had dated his oldest brother, Isaac, for two whole years before he'd met and married Hazel.

Timothy was pleased that Mary Lou had finally married Jacob, one of his other brothers. All his older brothers were now married, and he wondered how Taylor would fit in with his family if she agreed to marry him.

Taylor was so different, having been raised *Englisch*. The unfortunate thing was that she was still *Englisch* and more than anything he wanted her to join the community. He didn't see that happening, not really. She had shown some interest and had asked questions when she'd attended two of his brothers' weddings.

Timothy opened the lid of the dumpster, threw the trash inside, and took the empty trash basket back to Mary Lou. "Here you are," he said, dusting off his hands after he'd placed it by her feet.

"Well, don't just stand there, grab the vacuum cleaner."

"Vacuum cleaner?"

"You do have one, don't you? I thought since you have electricity here, you'd have a vacuum cleaner."

"Yes, I think I saw one once. Ah, it's in one of the bedrooms, I'm certain."

"Well fetch it. I'll move everything off the floor, and you vacuum."

He obeyed her command. Mary Lou was a kind woman, but she sure was bossy. He couldn't complain, though, since she was helping him. If it weren't for her encouragement, he didn't know when he would've gotten around to it.

As he dragged the vacuum cleaner from the bedroom into the living room, Mary Lou asked, "Have you seen Taylor lately?"

"I saw her last night. The sad thing is I only see

her now when she sneaks out of the house. Her parents hate me."

"Ah, that's not very good." Mary Lou kept picking things off the floor. There were odd socks, odd shoes and an assortment of video games.

"They haven't even met me and yet they hate me."

"I can understand their point of view, though, with all that's happened." She bent down and picked up the last thing—a pullover—and placed it on the couch with the collection of other things that she'd found.

He straightened the vacuum's power cord. "I guess. I thought they might want to get to know me, but they don't."

"They are probably upset, aren't they?" Mary Lou placed her hands on her hips.

"Furious." He nodded, looking around for the nearest power outlet. "They had to go overseas because they didn't know how to handle the situation."

"Are they back now?"

"They are. I'll get started now, shall I?"

"Yeah, I'll move on to the kitchen." Timothy plugged the vacuum cleaner in while feeling embarrassed that he'd left the place such a mess. He soon found the noise and the motion of the carpet cleaner rather soothing. After Timothy had turned the vacuum off, he looked at his handiwork. Never had he seen the place look that good. There had always been something on the floor, apart from the day he'd moved in with his friends. "That looks better already."

Mary Lou walked back into the room. "It does, and it didn't take long at all, did it?"

"No, it didn't."

"You find something to wipe down the coffee table and clean the windows, and I'll keep going in the kitchen."

He grimaced. "I hope you didn't get a fright when you went in there."

"I was expecting what I saw from the state of the living room."

An hour later they sat down.

"Thank you. I really appreciate you doing this for me."

Mary Lou shook her head and straightened her apron across her knees. It was a thing that older ladies did. "Now, what are we going to do with you?"

"What do you mean?"

"With you and Taylor and this *boppli* who is arriving soon?"

He clasped his hands together between his knees

and cast his gaze downward. "I'm not sure."

"Well, you still want to marry her, don't you?"

"More than anything."

"Good. You know what you want, so that is a positive thing. We just have to set a plan into motion to make it happen."

He was pleased that she was trying to be so positive and help him, but she just didn't know the situation and how difficult it was. "It's not as easy as that. You don't know how harsh her parents are and what they expect from her. You see, they're wealthy, and they wanted her to marry someone equally as wealthy, but then I came along and thwarted their plans. That's why they're so hostile. Taylor told me that they think her chances of achieving what they consider a good marriage are lessened now that she'll have a child soon."

"Well, they'll just have to change their ideas."

"That's why they're so upset. Their plans have been changed." He shook his head. "They aren't the kind of people who want to change their plans and I've forced them to do that. That's why they hate me, even though they've never met me. They hate the thought of me."

"Would they rather that this baby be born without Taylor being married?"

"I guess so. They certainly don't want her to be married to me. If I were a different man, I guess things would be different. They just don't like me being Amish—was Amish, will be Amish again. You know what I mean. I think Taylor's told them about that. Maybe she hasn't, and they don't like me just because I'm not from their social level."

"It's good to hear you intend on coming back to the community."

He looked down at the clean carpet, wondering how to make Mary Lou see how things were with the situation. She'd been out of the community for a good while some time back, so he might have a chance of making her understand. "The thing is, I can't dictate to her. I need to be guided by her. I can't force her to go into the community and I can't go back into the community without my child. Can you understand that?"

"I can. As you know, I've never had a child, but I will hopefully one day and the most important thing in the world would be to have a *boppli*."

He saw her face as she talked about children. She was caring and kind. "You will make a great *mudder*, Mary Lou."

Her face lighted up. "Do you think so?"

"I know it."

CHAPTER 2

TAYLOR'S MOTHER and father had been overseas for several weeks, trying to figure out what to do with Taylor's situation. Only her parents would say that they thought better away from her when they were far removed from the situation. They meant geographically far removed. It was just an excuse for another vacation.

It was Taylor's mother's first morning back in the house, that is, after she'd had two days in bed recovering from the jet lag. Taylor sat across the dining room table from her mother that morning as they both drank coffee.

"How did you cope with everything here while I was gone?"

Taylor looked across at her mother. They had staff

to do everything. The only job Taylor had been given was to look after her mother's prized orchids, even though the gardener could've and should've done that, given that most of them had drooping brown leaves.

"Okay, I guess."

Her mother raised a quizzical eyebrow. "We'll soon find out. You can accompany me to the greenhouse."

Taylor huffed. "I did the best I could, but I'm not a horticulturist."

Her mother glared at her. "All you had to do was water them once a week."

"Once?"

"Yes. Did you water them at all?"

Taylor nodded enthusiastically. "I did."

Her mother sipped her coffee. "I could've had someone else do it. Maybe I should've." Her mother bounded to her feet and headed to the door and Taylor was right on her heels.

"I watered them."

Mrs. Edwards stepped into the greenhouse to see brown leaves and dying flowers. "Oh, Taylor! I can't believe they could be this bad in the short space of time I've been gone."

"You were gone for ages."

She turned to face Taylor. "How are you going to look after a child if you can't look after some plants?"

"A baby is different."

"They still need care. Babies need more looking after, that's what I'm worried about. Too bad people know now because you could've gone away and had the baby adopted. Nobody would ever need have known." She looked back at her orchids then walked along the row, touching some and giving distressed looks at others. Taylor figured she was seeing which ones might be able to be saved.

"I'm not giving my baby away. It's your grandchild, don't you have any feelings whatsoever?"

"If you were married and married to a respectable person it would be an entirely different matter. What man's going to look at you now? No decent man. Harvey Winchester was interested in you and you could've made an excellent marriage with him. He's a doctor now."

Taylor crossed her arms over her chest. "I don't want to marry a doctor and I never liked Harvey much. You're the one who likes Harvey."

"He's studying to be a surgeon, so that's even better. It's important you marry someone with as much money as us and Harvey's an excellent candidate. Then you'll know that you're not being married for your money. Now, you'll have to lower your expectations." Her gaze dropped to Taylor's large belly.

"I think I'd be able to figure it out."

"Well, what are your plans? Have you thought that far ahead?" Her mother drew her eyes away from Taylor to focus back on the brown plants.

"I'm having the baby and I'll continue to study. My life won't change too much."

"Don't think I'm going to look after the kid while you study."

"No, I've switched to online and I'm taking fewer subjects per term. It'll take me a little longer, but I'll get there eventually."

"You take it for granted that your father and I will support you financially. You don't realize what we do for you." She shook her head and looked away from her. "We should cut you off."

"You wouldn't!"

"That's what we should do." She looked back at her plants. "I wonder if Tim will be able to salvage them."

"Tim?"

"The gardener. Not that dreadful man you're thinking about."

"The 'dreadful man' is Timothy anyway, not Tim. And he's not dreadful. If you ever cared to meet him you'd see that for yourself."

Mrs. Edwards caressed one of the brown leaves. "They're over-watered."

Taylor felt bad. She didn't remember what her mother told her about them. "I didn't know."

"I said once a week. You didn't listen."

"Why don't you have them on an automatic watering system? Everything else around here is automated."

"I like to nurture them myself. I don't know if any of them will survive."

"You shouldn't have gone overseas then."

"I had to get away. You've upset your father deeply. The doctor had to give him more blood pressure medication."

"And I suppose you had to have more sleeping pills?"

"That's right. Not that you'd care."

"Mom, that's not fair. I care about you and Dad, but I will have this baby and raise him myself, or her."

"That's something we'll talk about another day."

Taylor put her hand over her belly. It seemed her mother didn't realize how far along she was. It was only two weeks to her due date, and today she had an appointment with her doctor and, something else her mother did not know, Timothy was going to be there.

TIMOTHY WAITED across the road from the doctor's office. When he saw Taylor arrive, he made himself wait until the car drove off, and then he headed to meet her. His heart pounded. He hadn't been able to sleep, he was so excited to see her again. He walked in to see her sitting down and hurried to sit next to her and then he kissed her on her cheek. She grabbed his hand.

"I'm nervous," she whispered.

"Me too."

Taylor giggled. "Why are you nervous?"

"Everything."

They were called in to see the doctor. Timothy sat while Taylor was poked and prodded and hearts were listened to. He imagined how different this all would've been had she been Amish and had a midwife. Most of their babies were born at home, the way it should've been. Not in a sterile hospital environment. The only Amish women who chose a hospital birth were some who were having their first or the ones who might have had complicated births. He knew Taylor wouldn't have wanted to have her baby at home, not at her parents' place.

They were told that all was well. The meeting with the doctor barely took ten minutes, and Timothy hoped he'd be able to spend the rest of the afternoon with Taylor. Once they were outside, he asked, "What time do you have to be home?"

She smiled at him. "Anytime."

"Good."

"Do you have to go back to work?"

"Not today. I've taken the afternoon off. I start my second job at six tonight."

"You must be exhausted."

"I'm not." He shook his head. "Let's take a walk in the park." Hand in hand they walked down to the end of the block where there was a gateway through to a park. "We need to be together, agreed?"

She nodded. "I agree."

Things between them had progressed in these last weeks and now Taylor admitted she had feelings for him. However, they still had to meet in secret.

"If I come up with a plan for us to be together, will you follow it?"

"No. We'll both come up with a plan together. We need to work as a team."

He nodded. She was a modern woman and an *Englischer*. He had to tread carefully. "Agreed."

"How will we be together?"

"You could marry me. I know we've talked about it before, but the baby is so close now. I want us to be married before the birth and there's not much time left. We need to act now. I know I've asked before, but I'll ask again. Taylor, will you marry me?"

Taylor's face lit up. "Let's elope."

He rubbed his chin. "As in, run away and get married?"

"Run away, yes. Run away from everything and everyone. Far, far away." She giggled.

"That sounds good."

She pulled him toward a white bench and they sat down. "The running away part, or the getting married?"

"Both." He searched her face. "Do you mean it?"

She nodded and gripped his hand tighter. "I do."

"That's the greatest news that I have ever heard in my whole life. One thing is stopping us from running away, though."

"What's that?"

"If I were to run away just by myself, it wouldn't matter, but with you and our baby, we need money."

"Don't worry. I've got plenty of money."

"We can't use your money. I'm the man, the provider."

She let out a frustrated sigh. "That's an out-dated concept."

"Not in my lifetime. I need to be the provider. It would make me feel good to provide for you and our baby. It's the way it was meant ..." He stopped himself. "It's how I am and I'm never going to change. I want to look after you."

"That's all very well and good, but with your debts and paying that high rent I don't know how you're going to get out of the whole debt cycle you're in. Do you know how much money you'll have to make to cover your debts, and also have enough money for the three of us to live? And I'm not talking about living comfortably. How much will we need just to get by?"

"I don't know. I'm not that good at math. I failed at school." He was embarrassed to admit it, but Taylor needed to know his shortcomings as well as his good points.

Taylor squirmed to get more comfortable. "Why don't we get married in Florida? We'll stay away until the baby's born. It's only a couple of weeks away. And then when we come back married and with the baby, my parents will see things differently."

Timothy wished things could be that easy. "I've got to worry about my two jobs and paying the lease on the apartment."

"Just leave the apartment and the jobs."

He shook his head. He wasn't raised to let people down. "That would be irresponsible and not a good way to start our life together."

"Just do something irresponsible for once in your life, will you? That's the only way we can be together. You're so frustrating sometimes." She dropped his hand and inched away from him. "You're either going to have to let someone down, or we'll have to live off our parents. We can't have it both ways."

He moved closer to her. "Okay, I'll do it. Let's run away and get married, and we'll stay away until we have the baby." She was right. He had to throw caution to the wind and grasp hold of the opportunity now that Taylor was agreeable to marry him, at last.

"And then we'll figure out the rest after that. And don't worry about money just for the moment. We can live on my money. The important thing is that we're all together, isn't it?"

He nodded. "More than anything, that's what I want."

"And that's how it was always meant to be. We have to move quickly because with the baby being so close, the birth could happen at any time. I've done some looking into things and since we're not residents of Florida, we can get our wedding license and get married the same day."

He ran a hand through his dark hair, pleased she'd already had the thought in mind. "Let's do it. It's a long drive, so we had better get started."

"I'll arrange a car and a driver."

Timothy muttered, "I've got my job starting again at six."

"Forget it and the other one. We both decided that it's important we stay together, right?"

Timothy nodded even though his gut was churning. He'd never let anyone down deliberately.

"We also said that being together is more important than your job."

He nodded and pushed his doubts away. "It's more important than anything. More important than both my jobs."

"Exactly, so pack a bag. I'll go home and get some

things and then I'll meet you at your place. Then, we'll go from there."

Timothy said, "Can we really do this? It won't be the wedding you've dreamed of."

"I never dreamed of a wedding because I never thought I'd get married. Come on. You're the one who wanted to do this. You asked me, remember? We need to run away to be together, that's the only way."

He drew in a deep breath. "Okay. Let's do it."

CHAPTER 3

MARY LOU KISSED JACOB GOODBYE, and when he walked out the door, she turned around to face Magnolia's sullen face. In an effort to be a good Christian and a good woman of God, Mary Lou had extended an invitation to her cousin to visit the community again. Magnolia needed a husband and Mary Lou had agreed to help her find one. Being a wife and mother would calm Magnolia down. Getting married had changed Mary Lou for the better. Mary Lou thanked God every day that Jacob loved her. He had been the most eligible Amish bachelor for miles around, and he chose her. She didn't think it possible, but every day she grew even more in love with him.

"I'm glad he's gone. Now you can tell me who you

found to match me with. And don't say Benjamin Fuller, because he's far too young."

Mary Lou giggled at the thought of Magnolia with the young and carefree Benjamin. On her last visit, Magnolia had been outrageous, spreading rumors that she was dating Benjamin, along with doing other dreadful things. Yes, having a relationship of her own was what Magnolia needed. "I wouldn't have thought Benjamin would be good for you anyway. All the Fullers are now out of the question." Mary Lou walked to the kitchen to finish cooking breakfast for herself and Magnolia. As she moved the eggs around in the pan, she asked, "What about someone older, a man with *kinner* already?"

"*Nee*. I'm not going to take leftovers. How could I be sure he's not just after someone to take care of the *kinner* and the *haus?*" Magnolia sat heavily on one of the six chairs around the kitchen table.

"I'm talking about a specific widower. There's James Wilkinson. He's got two girls, and his *fraa* died around two years ago."

"*Nee*. Who else?"

Mary Lou slid the eggs onto two plates. "You dismissed him pretty quickly. Do you even know him?"

"I think so. I know who he is, anyway. He's got

light brown hair and he's clean-shaven." Magnolia scoffed. "He's looking for someone, with that clean-shaven face of his." Magnolia rolled her eyes.

"He is looking for someone and so are you. It's nothing to be ashamed of."

She shook her head. "He's too old."

"He's actually not that much older than you."

Mary Lou placed a plate in front of Magnolia.

"Is James the best you've come up with?"

"I have had a lot on my mind lately."

"Mary Lou, you promised me you'd find me a man to make up for stealing Jacob from me."

Mary Lou stared at her cousin in disbelief. "You never had Jacob in the first place, so how could I steal him from you?"

Magnolias eyes blazed, and for an instant, Mary Lou was sure she saw sparks fly out of them, and then her cousin's bottom jaw jutted out. "You told me he'd never be interested in me."

"I didn't think he would be."

"Because you wanted him for yourself, isn't that the truth? Why don't you admit it? You'll feel much better when you do."

Mary Lou sat down in front of her breakfast, wanting to tip the whole lot over Magnolia's head and watch it fall down her face. Instead, she took a deep breath and reminded herself she was a grown-up married woman, a Christian woman, and she had to show compassion, even to people who annoyed her. "Let's just move on. Jacob and I are married now, and I'm trying to find someone for you."

Magnolia picked up a fork and pushed the fried eggs around the plate. Mary Lou felt the pressure of everything she had to do as a new wife. How was she going to do everything? She was trying to focus on getting pregnant, keeping the house clean, making good meals for Jacob, fixing Timothy and Taylor's problems and, on top of that, she was supposed to find a man for her disagreeable cousin. And, as if that wasn't plenty, she had the pressure of showing the Fullers that Jacob had made a good choice in her. It was hard being Mary Lou! "Catherine and Samuel's wedding would be a perfect place to do some scouting around. There are always new visitors, relatives and such. Catherine could have a distant cousin who'd suit."

"I guess."

"Have you given any thought to what you are wearing to the wedding?"

"*Nee*. I'll just wear my Sunday best. Is it on this Saturday?"

"It is. Is your Sunday best the green one?"

"Jah." Magnolia studied Mary Lou's face. "What do you think I should wear?"

"Well, I was making a grape-colored dress to wear, but I can easily let it out for you. I'll make you a gift of it."

Magnolia eyes bugged out. "You mean take it in? I'm much smaller than you."

Mary Lou realized she'd spoken unwisely and Magnolia didn't realize she'd stacked on the weight. "Yeah, that's what I meant, take it in. Would you like that?"

Magnolia reached across the table and picked up a snippet of material. "Is this the color?"

"Yeah, that's it."

Magnolia face lighted up. "I'd love that, Mary Lou. *Denke.* I love your sewing. You could be a professional seamstress, and you'd be the best ever."

Mary Lou giggled. "I'm good at many things. I'll have it finished by the day before the wedding."

"I hope someone good will be there."

"Someone could be here already, right under your nose."

"Isn't that what you said about Samuel? And then he was pinched by Catherine from right under my nose." Magnolia sighed. "I've had no success with the Fullers. I need to try a different family."

"Yeah, I'm sorry about what happened with Catherine and Samuel. I had no idea they liked each other."

"Don't worry. It's not your fault."

Mary Lou was glad she'd showed patience just now. It had brought out a different side of Magnolia, a more reasonable side. "I think you'd be great as a *mudder* and James has got those two delightful girls."

"*Nee,* I want my own."

"If you married him, they would be yours."

Magnolia pouted. "You know what I mean."

"You could have your own as well."

Magnolia stared down at her eggs. "I suppose."

Mary Lou licked her lips. "If you're open to that idea, there is another widower. I just remembered him. He keeps to himself. He's got a girl who would be about eleven or twelve right now and a boy of around six."

"Who … How old is he? Younger would be better. I mean, younger than James."

"I'm not sure. We'll see who you get along with at the wedding. You never know who will be there."

"Okay, but what is the name of the one you just mentioned?"

"Gabe."

"How did his wife die?"

"Tragically, in a fire. A candle was left burning at night, and they think the curtains caught alight. They found her in the baby's room and she was most likely trying to get him out."

"Did the *boppli* get out?"

"*Jah,* his *shweschder* grabbed him on her way out and was yelling to her *mudder.* No one's sure what really happened. She could've fallen and was trapped."

"That's awful. It's so sad."

Mary Lou finished her mouthful of eggs. "Tragic. It really stunned the whole community."

"He must be a broken man."

"Yeah, everyone was devastated about it. And the six-year-old boy was the *boppli* then, so Gabe has been widowed for that long?"

"I'll meet him at the wedding—both of them. I'll keep an open mind and an open heart and let *Gott* find my one true love."

"*Jah,* that's the best way to think, Magnolia."

"Now, can you finish my dress today?"

Mary Lou laughed. "I'll work on it today, but I might not get it finished."

CHAPTER 4

TIMOTHY PUSHED the door of his apartment open. Taylor had gone back to her house to pack some things she needed for their elopement. There was nothing he needed in that apartment apart from a few items of clothing, which was just as well seeing that he was abandoning it.

Somebody would need to clear the apartment out and to do that would cost money. He sat down to write a note to his landlord, who lived in the apartment two doors down. He informed the landlord he'd repay all the cleaning costs and continue to pay the rent until the apartment was let. He thought that was only fair and he didn't want anyone to be out of pocket because of his sudden change of plans. He hoped the landlord would let him take what time he needed to pay off the debt he was about to incur.

Before he could forget, he hurried over to the landlord's apartment and slid the note under the door. Once he got back, he packed as much as he could in a backpack and waited at the front of the apartment building for Taylor, hoping she wouldn't change her mind.

When he saw the black car pull up in front of him, and Taylor's smiling face looking out at him, he knew he was doing the right thing. The driver got out and put his bag in the trunk and Timothy slid into the backseat beside Taylor. She grabbed his hand.

She brought his hand up to her face and kissed it. "Don't look so worried. This will work out fine."

Timothy said, "I'm not worried. This was how things were meant to be. We must always stay together." He lovingly touched her belly.

"We will. Nobody's going to force us apart. Even my parents respect marriage."

"That's good to hear. I'll always love you and take care of you. As soon as I can, when we get back, I'll get a better job that pays a lot more."

"Maybe we won't come back. Maybe we'll go somewhere else."

He didn't like the sound of never seeing his family again, but he had a new family now. Taylor and the baby were his new family. And he was the provider and the head of the new family. "I hope I can provide well for us." He scratched the back of his neck and kept silent about the money he already owed and the mounting debt he'd have on the apartment he'd just abandoned. Taylor must've read the worry on his face.

"Can you suddenly inherit something?"

He shook his head. "I'm the second-last son of seven, so it's not likely some distant relative's going to leave me a fortune." Timothy looked at the driver and wondered how Taylor secured him for such a long drive at such short notice. Was the big black car her parents'? Of course. It had to be. They were splitting the drive over two days, so surely her parents wouldn't be happy about one of their cars and drivers disappearing for four days.

AFTER AN OVERNIGHT STOP in a small roadside hotel and another day's worth of driving, the car stopped in front of a much grander hotel opposite the water.

"How are we going to pay for this?" Timothy regretted his question the instant it left his tongue. Taylor already said she'd pay, and he didn't want to keep talking about his money worries.

She got out of the car and waited for him to get out. "I told you I have money."

He stood in front of her on the pavement. "You mean your parents have money?" Again, the words slipped out of his mouth. *I really need to learn to think before speaking,* he thought.

"What's theirs is mine." Meanwhile, the driver placed their bags by their feet and then got back into the car. "We can't do this if you keep mentioning money every five minutes."

He shook his head and then picked up their bags. "Believe me, I'm trying not to. I'm just worried, that's all."

"We can go back if you want."

He chuckled. "No. We've come to get married, and that's what we'll do."

"Good."

"Let's get married now, today. We just passed a marriage chapel; let's go back there."

She giggled. "Okay. First, we need to check in here. I'll just tell the driver to go." She opened the front door of the car and spoke to the driver.

Timothy couldn't hear what was said; when she closed the door, the car pulled away.

"Where's he going?"

"Back home."

"Was that your parents' driver and their car?"

"One of the drivers and one of their cars. They won't even notice, trust me."

"How will we get back?"

"We're taking one day at a time, remember?"

He nodded and smiled, but it wasn't easy to slip into a life of spontaneity.

"Don't freak out on me now, Timothy."

"I'm not used to this one-day-at-a-time business, but I'll get used to it." He took a step toward the front door. "After you." He nodded his head to the door of the hotel.

Taylor handed over her credit card to the clerk behind the highly polished wooden reception counter when he asked for an imprint of it. They needed that imprint on record before they could be handed keys. After a few attempts at swiping her card, the clerk looked up at her. "I'm sorry, but this credit card isn't working."

"It does that sometimes. Can you please try again?"

As the clerk tried again, Timothy whispered to

her, "You only have that one credit card?"

"I have some cash too."

It bothered Timothy that Taylor, or rather Taylor's parents were paying for all of this. He was going to have to work two jobs for the rest of his life to pay for everything and to do that he would barely see anything of Taylor or the baby unless it was when they were sleeping. Still, it was a price he would pay to secure his family and keep them together.

He pushed all that to the back of his mind. It was the main and vital issue that their baby be born legitimately, with a married mother and father. It was the most important thing to him. He couldn't shake the upbringing with the deeply rooted rules and guidelines etched into his mind. Having a baby out of wedlock was not acceptable to him and he was glad he had managed to win Taylor over to the idea of marriage. She'd resisted for such a long time, and now she had admitted freely that she loved him.

The clerk smiled.

"Did it work this time?" Taylor asked him.

"It did." He smiled at them both. "Sign here." After she scribbled her signature, the clerk gave her the keys. "You're on the fourth floor."

"Overlooking the water, I hope."

"Yes."

"Perfect." She grabbed the keys, turned around and smiled at Timothy as they headed to the elevator. "When we get to the room, I think you have to carry me over the threshold. If you're strong enough to lift the both of us."

Timothy chuckled. "Of course I am. You're not marrying a weakling." The elevator doors opened and they found their room. He placed the bags down and unlocked the door, and then he swept her into his arms while she shrieked with laughter. He carried her through the open doorway and placed her back on her feet in the middle of the floor.

"I tricked you. It's after we're married you have to carry me."

He laughed and shook his head. "Well, what are we waiting for?" He pulled the bags into the room.

"I saw that the wedding chapel we passed said, 'No booking required.'"

"Ah, you saw it too. I like the sound of not having to book." He put out his hand. "Let's go get married."

CHAPTER 5

THEY WALKED into the wedding chapel and found a large lady in a light blue, polka-dot dress sweeping the floor. Her red hair was swept up into a French roll, and her make-up was impeccably applied. The only thing that marred her pristine appearance was the way that she was opening and closing her mouth while chewing gum.

"Excuse me, Ma'am, you are doing weddings today, aren't you?" Timothy asked.

"Sorry. We're finished today."

Taylor stepped closer. "Oh, I didn't know you closed so early. It says on the sign that you don't need a booking and it didn't say anything about times."

The woman's gaze fell on Taylor's large belly. "In

a hurry?"

"We're in a big hurry," Timothy said.

Taylor said, "Could you marry us now?" The woman shook her head until Taylor produced a hundred-dollar bill.

The woman's face lighted up when she saw the large note. "It'll be five hundred."

"Okay, take this as a tip. Can I pay on card?"

"Yes." She quickly snatched the note from her and said, "I'll tell the reverend. Do you both have identification and rings?"

"No, we don't have rings," Timothy said. "We do have ID."

"Don't worry; we have rings for six dollars."

"We'll take one," Taylor said. "Size six, please."

Five minutes later they stood in front of the reverend, who, they guessed, was the red-haired lady's husband. She was standing in as witness, bridesmaid, and best man. It wasn't the wedding Timothy had envisioned and he was even surer that it wasn't the wedding that the daughter of wealthy parents had ever thought she'd have. Timothy hoped that Taylor wouldn't regret marrying him in a few years.

Once Timothy and Taylor had repeated the vows, the reverend said, "Here's where you slip the ring on her finger." He waited while Timothy did so, and then continued, "You may kiss the bride."

Timothy leaned toward Taylor and gently kissed her on the lips.

"Mr. and Mrs. Fuller, you are now husband and wife. Congratulations," the reverend said, before he hurried away, presumably to finish his dinner.

"Now we just have some papers to sign, and you can be on your way," the woman said, putting her hands on their backs and pushing them to the back of the chapel.

WHEN THEY WERE outside in the afternoon sun, Timothy said, "Now we must have a nice dinner out somewhere."

"I know the best Italian restaurant."

"I love Italian food."

She pulled out her cell phone and a few seconds later had made a booking for seven that evening. "Let's take a walk."

They started walking along the beach but before long Taylor grew tired and needed to rest.

"There's a seat over there." Timothy held her hand and led her to the seat. They sat quietly for a while overlooking the calming waves.

"The water is so peaceful," Taylor said.

"It truly is. I can tell you I feel different being married."

"Do you?" she asked.

"I do. Now I don't have to worry about other men trying to steal you away. You're mine now forever."

She giggled. "You never had to worry about other men."

"You gave me a hard time there for a while."

"I never wanted to get married, that was why. I just couldn't see that for myself. I'm very independent."

He nodded. "I know, too independent, almost."

She rested her head on his shoulder. "Is that a problem?"

"It won't be, as long as you're not so independent that you don't need me."

"I will always need you and so will our baby." She put her hands on her belly, and Timothy touched her tummy and felt the baby move.

"That was a strong kick."

"I've been getting kicked badly today." She giggled.

"It must feel odd."

"It does. No one ever told me how uncomfortable it would be in these last weeks. It was different at the beginning when it was just a flutter and I wasn't sure if it's the baby moving or not." Taylor sighed. "Pregnancy is just something we women have to go through."

"That doesn't sound like something you'd say."

"It's not. It's what my mother always says. I think she regretted having me."

"Surely not. How can she regret God's greatest gift?"

Taylor roared with laughter. "I was in the way more than anything. They didn't want me. I was in the way of their social lives and their vacations. I saw more of nannies when I was growing up. I didn't have a proper relationship with my mother until I was a teenager."

Timothy shook his head. "Our baby will have a very different life."

"Yes, we'll make sure of that."

"Are you ready to walk back to the room to get ready for dinner?"

"Carry me?"

He stood up, took her hand and helped her up. "I'd carry you, but you're far too heavy."

She slapped him. "No more fat jokes."

He chuckled.

CHAPTER 6

AFTER THEY ATE their Italian dinner, they came home to their hotel room. "Is this where I have to carry you over the threshold?"

"I guess so, but we should've done that right after we got married."

"Yes, and before you ate all that food just now."

She playfully slapped his muscled shoulder. "You promised no more fat jokes."

Laughing, he swept her up into his arms. Although he was tall and had a normal build, he was strong from the laboring work he'd always done. It wasn't a problem for him to pick Taylor up, not even if she'd been twice the size. He carried her into the room and placed her gently down on the couch. "How was that?"

"Perfect, Mr. Fuller. You passed with flying colors."

"Good. I hope I will keep passing all your tests as the years go on."

"So do I."

It was four in the morning when Taylor shook Timothy awake. "I think I'm having contractions."

"Right now?" He had just woken up from a deep sleep and wondered if he was dreaming. When he realized he wasn't, panic set in.

"Yes now."

He sat bolt upright. "What? We can't have the baby here in Florida."

"That's what we decided."

He rubbed his head. "Did we?"

"Yes. Don't freak out on me now. We've got each other and I'm sure there's a hospital nearby." She placed her hand on her belly. "Tomorrow I was going to check out the hospital situation. I thought there was time."

Timothy jumped out of bed and paced up and down. "I'm here every step of the way." He grabbed the phone's receiver. "What do we do?"

"Call the nearest hospital and tell them we might

be coming in later."

"Why not now?" he asked, wishing he was better in a crisis.

"It takes a long time from the first contraction. Find out where the nearest hospital is that can deliver a baby."

He called the concierge and found out there was a hospital fifteen minutes away.

"That was another one," she said when he sat down on the bed beside her.

"Shall we go in now?" Timothy hoped he wasn't going to have to deliver the baby by himself.

"Okay. That one was close to the last one."

Timothy blew out a breath of relief.

IT WAS ONLY four hours after they'd arrived at the hospital, and Taylor was lying in the hospital bed with their baby girl in her arms.

Timothy stared down at his small daughter, his miracle. He'd been right by Taylor's side throughout the birth and he had a new respect for women and mothers. He'd loved the baby before she was born, but now his heart had opened even more. "She's so precious, Taylor."

"She's gorgeous."

"What will we call her?" Timothy asked.

"What about Mary Lou after your lovely sister-in-law?"

He shook his head. "No, please, definitely not."

"Why?"

"I like Mary Lou, a lot even, but I would prefer to call our daughter by a name that is uniquely hers, or at least not after anyone we know."

"Okay. I'll have to think on it. Unless you've got ideas?"

"Miranda?"

"Miranda Fuller. Hmm, I was thinking something more like Ruby."

"No. I like that, but it doesn't suit her."

Taylor looked down at her daughter. "She does look a little like a Miranda. Miranda, it is, then. Miranda Lou Fuller, okay? With Lou as her middle name."

"Are you sure? It sounds good to me."

Taylor nodded. "I'm sure."

CHAPTER 7

AFTER TWO DAYS and nights in the hospital, Timothy, Taylor and the baby headed back to the hotel. Timothy called home to tell them the baby had been born. Benjamin answered the phone and said he'd pass it on and let everyone know.

"How much did that all cost?" Timothy asked in the backseat of the taxi, well aware that Taylor had paid on her credit card.

"It doesn't matter. I've taken care of it."

"I wish I could've."

"Does it worry you?"

He sighed. "I guess it does. I'm trying not to think about things like that. I know you get upset when I worry about money. Everyone needs it to live."

She nodded. "I know." She passed Miranda to him. "Just worry about this little one and leave the rest to me."

He smiled as he took the baby into his arms.

JUST AS TIMOTHY had handed the baby to Taylor so he could unlock the hotel door, he heard Taylor's cell phone that they'd left in the room. He hurried to answer it and just as he reached it, it stopped. He picked it up, stared at the screen and then turned to Taylor. "That was your mother. It says you've had eighteen missed calls."

Taylor shook her head. "I'll have to call her back."

"Does she know where we are? Did you leave her a note or anything?"

Taylor nodded. "I left a note in my bedroom."

"And? What did it say?"

"I just wrote that I was running away with you."

"And marrying me?"

"Uh-huh." Taylor nodded.

Timothy placed her cell phone back down on the table. "They must be furious."

"I'd reckon they would be." Taylor passed the baby back to Timothy. "I'll call her back."

"I'll take Miranda into the bedroom to give you

some privacy." Timothy walked into the bedroom, placed the sleeping newborn down in the middle of the king-sized bed, and then lay down next to her. Nothing mattered now that he had Taylor and the baby with him. People could hate him and he didn't care. He didn't want to hear the conversation between Taylor and her mother because Mrs. Edwards had made such grand plans for Taylor, and then Taylor had ruined it all by marrying him.

As he lay with closed eyes and with his fingertips gently touching the baby, he listened to Taylor tell her mother that she had the baby and all was well. The next five minutes were filled with Taylor answering all her mother's questions because all he heard was Taylor replying with a yes or a no. Then he heard Taylor raise her voice. "No, you can't do that. We're in Florida. How will we get home?"

This was one of the things Timothy had feared. He knew they were cutting off their daughter's credit card. He would have to call his parents and ask for the fare home.

He knew something would work out because they were married and Miranda had arrived safely into the world. He didn't like to hear his wife upset, so he walked to the door to mouth to her to calm down. And just at that moment she ended the call from her mother and threw the phone across the room. It landed against a wall and crashed on the white tiled floor.

He walked over and picked up the phone. Miraculously, it wasn't broken. He placed it back on the table in the center of the room. "Everything will work out. Isn't that what you're always telling me?"

Taylor crossed her arms over her chest. "They're cutting off my credit card."

"It was obvious that was going to happen. Don't worry about it."

"You don't understand. It was linked to a trust fund my grandparents set up for me. They can't do this. It's my money."

"They must think they can."

"Technically they can. They can freeze that money until I'm twenty-five and that's years away."

It pleased him a little to learn that it hadn't been her parents' money. "Can we get home?"

Slowly she nodded. "I do have cash. It'll be enough for us to get home."

"Good." He looked around the hotel. "We'll leave first thing in the morning. We can't stay another night in this expensive place."

"We'll have to go by bus, and it'll be a dreadful journey. Mom said I couldn't use her car."

"We'll make the best of it. You can sleep on my shoulder and Miranda will be okay."

"Buses are cramped and horrible."

"They might be all that, but we'll be together." He stretched out his hand, and she took hold of it. "Come and look at Miranda." He led her into the bedroom and Taylor smiled when she saw the tiny baby on the king-sized bed. "We might have had a rocky beginning, but we'll get through it, and now we're a family."

She smiled and rested her head on his shoulder. "All we need is each other."

CHAPTER 8

THEY USED NEARLY all of Taylor's remaining cash getting a taxi from the bus station to Timothy's apartment.

"I just have to hope that Norman hasn't let my apartment out yet." He thought there would be a chance he hadn't since they hadn't even been gone a week.

They got out of the taxi at his old apartment complex and while he was pulling the bags out of the trunk, Taylor paid the driver. He walked to the door of his apartment with Taylor holding the baby and following close behind. He stuck his key in the lock and was surprised that it turned. He said over his shoulder, "He hasn't changed the locks yet, that's a good sign." He slowly opened the door and saw the apartment just as he'd left it.

He opened the door fully allowing Taylor to walk through. "Everything's just as I left it. You wait here, and I'll talk with the landlord two apartments over. I won't be long."

Taylor looked around and sat down on the couch holding their baby. As fast as he could, Timothy walked to the apartment where Norman lived and knocked on the door. After a while, his wife Monique opened the door.

"Hello, Timothy. I'm surprised to see you back. I got your note."

"I can see you haven't leased the apartment out yet."

"Norman's been away working and I haven't had a chance to do anything about it."

So much was riding on the outcome of this conversation. If he couldn't live back in his apartment, where would they go? "I've had a change of plans."

"Do you want to come back?"

"I do if that's all right. I know I'm a little behind, but I'll catch up."

"I know. I was going over the bookwork just as you knocked on the door."

Taylor appeared behind him and handed her over two hundred dollars. "Taylor, can we spare it?"

Before she could answer the notes were plucked from Taylor's hands.

"Thank you. This will allow you to stay until you catch up with your back rent. Norman's away for a couple more weeks, and he'll sort things out when he gets back."

"Thank you, Monique."

"Is that all?" She looked at Taylor and the baby.

"Yes. Er, this is my wife, my brand-new wife, Taylor, and our baby Miranda."

"There'll be two of you staying there and a baby?"

"That's right."

Monique nodded and Timothy could see the wheels turning over in Monique's brain. Was she going to charge more rent? "When I first came here I had two housemates, so nothing's really changed."

Monique nodded again, and then Timothy turned around and gently guided Taylor away from his landlord's apartment.

"Thank you for that, Taylor. Do we have enough money for food? I mean I have a little, but is yours all gone?"

"I have fifty dollars left." They walked back inside Timothy's apartment—their apartment, now.

"I'll have to see if I can get both my jobs back. I don't think they'll be happy to see me because I didn't show up and didn't call them."

"Timothy, we need those jobs. Just do what you can to get them back. Go now, I'll have a little sleep. Miranda will sleep soon."

"One will be closed, but I'll head off and talk to the manager of my night job." He was actually fairly confident he would get those jobs back, but he didn't want to get Taylor's hopes up in case he was mistaken. He had changed jobs fairly frequently and these two were both casual jobs with high pay. It needed to be high pay with his debts and the rent he was paying for the apartment. It was convenient that he'd never replaced those housemates.

It was a two-mile walk into town to see about getting his job back. He met with his manager and gave him a story that was mostly true about suddenly getting married and having the baby. The manager accepted what he said and he was able to work that very night.

He arrived home in the early hours of the morning, exhausted and needing sleep. Without changing his clothes or showering, he collapsed onto the spare bed and turned his alarm on for six in the morning.

He'd have to do some fast talking to make sure he hadn't lost his day job.

When his alarm sounded, he wrote Taylor a note saying he'd bring food home and he'd be back around five or six, if he were successful at keeping his daytime job. It was hard to leave Taylor and Miranda, but he had to keep the money coming in. And it was only a matter of time before his parents found out about the marriage, and just like Taylor's parents, he knew they wouldn't be pleased.

AFTER TAYLOR HAD FED MIRANDA, bathed her and dressed her in a clean set of clothes, she sat down on the couch to feed her. Would they ever be able to buy her a crib, and all those other things that people bought their babies? She had newborn sized clothing that she'd purchased some time ago before she knew if she was having a boy or a girl. Now that she had a girl, all she wanted to do was go to the stores and spend big on a shopping spree and buy pink baby clothing and accessories. It was awful to think about raising the baby in the drab apartment that smelled vaguely of sweaty boys and days-old take-out.

She couldn't go out anywhere because then she would spend money and she was trying to avoid that. She'd found the note hanging on the fridge, telling her that Timothy was bringing food home. At least there were staples there, such as bread in the freezer, and canned food.

Taylor looked at the clock. Ten thirty in the morning and Timothy wasn't back. "I think your daddy has kept both of his jobs, Miranda."

Miranda was feeding and then she started to close her eyes. For now, it was okay for her to sleep on a bed because she didn't move much and couldn't roll over. What would happen in a few weeks' time when she was bigger? There were so many things Miranda needed and it bothered Taylor that Timothy couldn't provide them.

She wondered how her life would be different if she'd stayed with her parents and had never run away to get married. Once her parents saw how precious Miranda was, they would've spoiled her and she would've had the best of everything.

Eloping had seemed like a good idea at the time, but now she wondered if she would spend her whole life in poverty scrimping and saving to make ends meet.

All day she'd spent watching the clock, and when

she heard the key in the door, she ran to it and opened it. Timothy smiled at her and held his two bags of groceries higher.

"I've come with food."

"Fresh vegetables and fruit I hope."

"Yes, real food."

He put the bags down in the kitchen and Taylor wrapped her arms around him. "I've missed you so much."

"Me too. Can you make me something to eat? I've got to shower and get to my next job."

"You're working again tonight?"

"Yes. My night job is most nights unless I ask for a night off or they're closed for some reason."

"I was hoping we could watch a movie together tonight and relax."

He kissed her on the cheek and stepped back. "That sounds good, but I can't." He headed to the bathroom.

All day she'd waited and now she was faced with more time alone. When she heard the shower turn on, she sifted through the food so she could make him a meal. With no time for vegetables to cook, all she could think of was a ham and salad sandwich. Cooking wasn't a strong point of hers.

She placed the sandwiches on the table and sat

and waited for Timothy to finish his shower. Then she heard him talking to Miranda.

"The dinner's on the table. You'll have to eat now if you don't want to be late," she called out.

He walked out of the bedroom pulling on his clothes. "I know. How was she today?"

"As perfect as ever."

He sighed. "I wish I could spend more time with her."

"Me too."

Timothy sat, ate his meal and then he was gone. Taylor washed the dishes and finished putting away the rest of the shopping.

TEN DAYS LATER, nothing had changed for Taylor, and every day was the same. She was frustrated with only seeing Timothy for half an hour a day, spending long days by herself, and having to stay home because of the money situation.

She knew she had to have a serious talk with Timothy. If she went home now her baby would have the best of everything.

· · ·

THAT NIGHT when Timothy came home, she sat him down for a conversation.

"It's not working, Timothy. I can't live like this. I have to go back home. I see that as the only option. I'll go home for a short time and then see—"

"Home? This is our home now." This was the worst thing he could possibly hear. He'd managed to get his apartment back and his two jobs. Didn't she see how hard he was working? He wasn't doing it for himself.

"It's not, it's not our home. I know everyone thinks I'm spoiled and you probably do too. I don't want or need the baby to have the best of everything, but I do want her to have something."

The words cut deep into Timothy's heart. He was trying the best he could to provide for her and the baby and to keep everyone happy. It all seemed an impossible task. It was like he'd been juggling ten balls in the air and he knew that sooner or later it would all fall apart. Some and maybe all of those balls would drop. The time had come. "What do you want to do? You must have a plan."

"I think I should go home and—"

"Will they have you?"

Taylor nodded. "I think they will. I'm here every day by myself and I'm lonely. Miranda will need things as time goes on. New clothes and she doesn't even have a crib."

"And we'll have the money by then. Things are tight now because most of the money is getting us out of debt."

"I'm not in debt, you are."

He sat back and looked at her. Didn't she understand that they were a team? "Taylor, I'm doing what's best for this family."

She shook her head. "I can't do this. I can't live here." She looked around.

"I know it's not much, but ..."

"And I can't live on promises."

"I don't want you to. If we get through this, we'll have a lot to look forward to." He gulped. He didn't want to lose them and he was doing everything in his power to keep them. It seemed nothing he did was good enough. He couldn't think of a way to keep her there.

"I'll go back home just until things get sorted out, okay?"

No, it wasn't okay, but he couldn't keep her there like some kind of hostage if she was unhappy. "When will you be back?"

"When you're able to provide. Maybe when you're out of debt."

"I know the situation's not ideal, but if we just stick together things will work out."

She shook her head. "I just wanted us to be together, but I never see you, so what difference does it make if I'm at my parents' house?"

He stared at her in disbelief, knowing that this was the beginning of the end.

"I'm calling Mom now. Don't worry, we're not over. I'm just going to live at home for a while."

After Taylor called her mother, they sent a car for her.

Soon after, he watched his baby and his wife drive away. At least he knew where Taylor and the baby would be and that they'd be safe, but in his heart, he knew that Taylor was disappointed in him and he was even more upset with himself.

CHAPTER 9

TIMOTHY WORKED Sunday morning and when he knew that Mary Lou and Jacob would be home from the Sunday meeting, he went to their house. Jacob was out, but Mary Lou invited him to sit on the porch. There they sat drinking lemonade.

Timothy could no longer hold it in, and unburdened his sad tale onto his sister-in-law. He finished by saying, "So, she's gone home to her parents' and they hate me."

"They only hate you because they don't know you, Timothy."

"I don't know what to do about that."

"Go and see them."

"I can't. They'd throw me out before they'd let me get two words out."

"At least they'd respect you for trying and going and introducing yourself. If they don't hear from you at all, they'll think there's something wrong with you—think there's something fishy about you."

"I never thought about things that way. I think you're right."

"Well, clean yourself up, go have a shower and put on your best clothes, and go speak with them."

He looked down at himself in the clothes that he hadn't had a chance to wash. He had one clean set of clothes left. "Okay, I'll do it."

"Now?"

"I think around seven this evening is when they'll both be home, seeing it's a Sunday—both Mr. and Mrs. There's the other part to the problem."

"The money?"

Timothy nodded. "My debts. Taylor keeps calling them 'my debts.'"

"They are yours. Anyway, fix one problem at a time."

"All right."

TIMOTHY GOT out of the taxi, parted with his money sadly, took a deep breath, and looked up at the huge white house. He walked up the gravel driveway and then knocked on the door.

To his surprise, Taylor opened it. She stepped through the door and closed it behind her. "What are you doing?"

"How's Miranda?"

"She's good, but you know I can't ask you in. My parents are home."

"I've come to talk to them."

"They won't speak to you."

"It doesn't matter; I must have my say and convince them that I'm a decent person who only wants the best for you and Miranda."

"They don't care about that. They only care about money and social standing. You have neither."

Mary Lou's words about respect flashed back through his mind. He might have nothing and be nobody, but he was going to stand there and tell them that he would look after Taylor and their child as best he could. He might be struggling a bit now, but he'd tell them that would change very shortly.

"Okay." She shook her head. "It's suicide, but I'll tell them you're here."

"You look lovely, by the way."

She giggled. "I look dreadful."

"You're beautiful."

She leaned forward and kissed his lips. "I'll say goodbye now because I know this won't end well. Call me after."

"I'll call you at ten tonight. I can call you at that time when I'm working, too, because that's when I get my break."

Taylor left him standing at the door and very soon he was faced with Taylor's mother and father, who looked more than a little grim.

"You want to talk with us?" Taylor's mother stood rigidly with her arms by her side.

"Yes, if I could."

Mr. Edwards put his hand up. "You're not coming into our home. You can say what you've got to say right there."

"I want to tell you that I love Taylor and our baby and I will do my best to provide for them."

"You've ruined Taylor's life, do you know that?" Mr. Edwards said.

"I only want the best for her and our baby."

"And you think you're the best?" Taylor's father looked him up and down as if he was a clod of dirt.

"I don't think I'm the best, but I think I am the best for Taylor because she loves me. I might not have much at the moment, but I have big plans for a bright future for the three of us. Together we will build a future."

"And what was the meaning of you sneaking off and getting married?"

"At the time, we saw that as the only way that we could be together. My parents were against us getting married just as much as the both of you."

Taylor's mother folded her arms across her chest. "Why would your parents be against the marriage?"

"My parents are Amish."

"What?" she screeched. "Oh, this just gets better."

"Leave us alone. You'll not see Taylor or the baby again." Taylor's father pulled his wife inside and slammed the door in his face.

Timothy turned and walked away. That was exactly the response he'd expected, but because he was expecting the reaction it didn't upset him too much. He walked away hoping Taylor wouldn't be too upset by her parents' shouting. It was a four-mile walk before he found a bus that would take him close to home.

By the time Timothy reached his apartment, he was distraught. He unlocked the door of his apartment and sat heavily on the couch. What if they brainwashed Taylor and made her stay away from him? A marriage certificate didn't mean much if they were living in separate places.

Timothy closed his eyes and for the first time in a long time he prayed. He poured his heart out and asked for forgiveness for ignoring God for so long. He had to get his life back together and he figured the only way was to turn back to God and put Him first in his life.

CHAPTER 10

Timothy was so upset he needed to talk with someone. He used part of his allotted weekly grocery money and headed back to Mary Lou's house. Perhaps he'd even get there in time for the evening meal.

Mary Lou opened the door as soon as the taxi pulled up. She waited for him by the open door and as he approached, delicious food smells wafted under his nose.

"Did you speak with them?"

He walked up the porch steps. "*Jah*. It didn't go well at all."

"Oh, I'm sorry to hear that. Have you eaten?"

"*Nee*."

"You're just in time for the evening meal if you'd like to join us."

"*Denke.* I would, very much." He walked into the kitchen to see that Jacob was already seated at the table.

"Mary Lou told me about your problems," Jacob said.

"Which ones? All of them?" He chuckled trying to make light of his situation.

Jacob said, "Just leave things be at the moment. The way I see it, it's time that'll take care of the problem."

"Normally, I'd agree, but every day that passes is a day I don't see Miranda. I talked to her parents like you suggested, Mary Lou." Jacob looked over at Mary Lou, and Timothy added, "I couldn't have done without Mary Lou and her support during this whole thing and she was great talking with Taylor months back."

Mary Lou placed a bowl of mashed potatoes on the table.

"She's *wunderbaar,*" Jacob said, "that's why I married her."

"*Jah,* well, don't forget it." Mary Lou said with a laugh as she hurried to put more food on the table.

"I won't because you'll remind me," Jacob said, which made Mary Lou giggle.

Magnolia burst into the room. "What did I miss? Oh, it's you, Timothy."

"*Jah,* it's me." Timothy didn't know Magnolia would be there. He had thought he'd be able to get some advice, but now he felt he couldn't be so open about his problems.

"What's going on?" Magnolia looked at everyone in turn.

Timothy cleared his throat. "I ran away with Taylor and got married."

"Great!"

"*Nee,* it's not great because I've got no money. We were using her credit card until her parents found out and stopped the money. Although, technically it was her money. Then we only had enough cash to make it back here and meanwhile, I'd chucked my jobs and my apartment. I had to get them back. My work schedule and the horrible apartment were too intolerable for Taylor to bear, so she's taken the baby and moved back in with her folks." He drew a breath. So much for keeping things to himself.

"Oh no!" Magnolia shook her head. "I'm so sorry. Women can be so awful sometimes."

"It's not her fault. She's used to a certain lifestyle. I managed to talk my way back into my jobs. So, I can pay down my debts, anyway. But that means I'm away at one job or the other, except for sleeping when I can."

Magnolia shook her head. "You've got debts?" Timothy nodded and Magnolia sat down next to him. "There's only one thing you can do."

"What's that?"

"You'll have to come back to the community, straighten out your life with *Gott* before anything *gut* can happen in your life."

Mary Lou finished placing the food on the table and she sat down next to Jacob.

"I know you're right, Magnolia. I've resisted that for so long because I'm scared *Gott* will have other plans that don't include Taylor or my *boppli*."

Magnolia shook her head. "*Gott* gives us the desires of our hearts, and what's your heart's desire?"

"Taylor and the *boppli* to be with me and for us to be a family."

Magnolia raised her hands in the air. "Problem solved."

Timothy chuckled. "I wish it was as simple as that."

Jacob said, "We should give thanks for the food

before it gets cold." They all closed their eyes and said their silent prayer of thanks. When they were done, Jacob continued, "You know, Timothy, it might be as simple as what she's saying."

Timothy bit his lip. "What do you think, Mary Lou?"

"I came back to the community and even suffered being shunned. You won't be shunned, Timothy, because you've never officially joined by baptism."

"I know I won't be shunned and I'm not worried about that. I'm worried about losing Taylor."

Mary Lou nodded. "I was just trying to make a point. If it were me, I'd return, but you have to make your own decision and be comfortable with it."

"Or make it by faith," Magnolia suggested.

Timothy sighed. "I feel I'm losing her now anyway, and I'm doing everything in my own strength. Maybe you're right, Magnolia, and I should rely on *Gott's* strength."

"Undoubtedly."

Timothy stared at Magnolia, wondering when she'd become this wise. And why wasn't she applying it to her own life? He'd heard of the trouble she'd tried to create between Samuel and Catherine on her last visit.

Magnolia spooned a mound of potatoes onto her

plate and then passed them to Timothy. "Also, why don't you move home and save money on rent?"

"I was considering doing just that. I mean, if I come back to the community it only makes sense to live with my folks."

"I could help you move all your things back," Jacob offered.

"It's okay. All I have is a few items of clothing. The furniture was already there."

CHAPTER 11

IT WAS TWO DAYS LATER. Mary Lou and Magnolia were borrowing a spool of grape-colored cotton thread from Mrs. Fuller to finish Magnolia's dress for the wedding when Timothy arrived in a taxi.

He sat his mother and father down in the kitchen and asked them if he could come home. Mary Lou tried not to listen in, but then she heard shrieks from Mrs. Fuller about him being married.

Mary Lou was sitting in the living room with Magnolia when Mrs. Fuller came out of the kitchen followed closely by Timothy.

Benjamin walked into the house whistling, without a care in the world. He stopped still when he saw his mother looking distraught and Timothy following her.

Timothy pointed to Benjamin. "I called Benjamin and told him I got married and that the baby was born. He said he'd tell everyone."

Mrs. Fuller narrowed her eyes at Benjamin. "Benjamin, you knew?"

Benjamin scratched his head. "Knew what?"

Mrs. Fuller said, "Why didn't you tell us your *bruder* got married?"

"Oh, I forgot." He chuckled. "Looks like you know now."

Mrs. Fuller's hands balled into fists and she shrugged with rage. "You're impossible, Benjamin."

"Why am I in trouble? I'm not the one who ran away and got married. I've been the good and faithful son who's always been here giving you no trouble."

Timothy said, "It's true. I'm the one who's the family disappointment, the sheep who's gone astray, the weak link, the duck among the swans."

Mrs. Fuller's lips downturned and she rushed out of the room and headed up the stairs. Benjamin hurried after her and stood at the bottom of the stairs. "At least Timothy didn't have the child out of wedlock. Aren't you happy about that?"

"You've upset her good and proper, Timothy," Magnolia said from the couch.

Benjamin turned away from the stairs. "I don't know why if he's married now."

Timothy shook his head. "It's not the right thing in *Mamm's* eyes. Taylor's not in the community for one thing."

"Especially now that there is a child involved. That's why she's upset." Magnolia said.

Mary Lou frowned at Magnolia, stood and walked over to the brothers. "I'll have a talk with her and try to make her see that it's not as bad as she thinks."

Magnolia jumped to her feet. "Me too. Although, I don't think it's my place to offer an opinion, in a way, but I'll try to help make her feel better." Magnolia looked at the boys as though waiting for their approval.

"Okay, calm her down please," Timothy said.

"You go first," Magnolia said to Mary Lou.

"*Nee*, we'll go together." Mary Lou hoped Magnolia would be on her best behavior. When she wanted to, her cousin could give good common sense advice.

Together they walked up the stairs and knocked on Mrs. Fuller's bedroom door. "Can we come in?" Mary Lou asked. "It's Magnolia and Mary Lou."

"*Jah*," a weak voice replied.

Mary Lou pushed the door open and saw her mother-in-law wiping her eyes.

"Are you all right, Ivy?" Magnolia asked her.

"I'm trying to be. I can't help being extremely upset. He's married and didn't tell any of us. He's ruined his life and now he can't even marry within the community. It's a lot for a *mudder* to take in. I just wanted the best for all my sons."

"He's trying to fix things," Magnolia said. "He's quite worried."

"Mary Lou, you already know this. Our family has always had a good name, and now that's just not the way it is."

Magnolia said, "*Jah,* your family has a good name even as far away as in my community."

"Your community's not that far," Mary Lou reminded Magnolia, wishing she'd keep quiet for just one minute.

Mrs. Fuller continued, "People avoid me now. I no longer get invited to the quilting bees or to organize the charity functions. People look down when I walk by."

"Not everyone, surely," Magnolia said.

"But don't you see, Magnolia, nobody did that to us before. It's the same with Obadiah. He never says anything, but I know he's suffering from the shame of it all."

"Obadiah?" Magnolia asked.

"That's Mr. Fuller," Mary Lou said. "Isn't it good that Timothy and Taylor are married now?"

"Still, how it happened is not a good thing, and nobody will forget that, Mary Lou. Everybody will remember even if Taylor were to join our community."

"Well, if people like to think that way, don't worry about them. You can't help what your son has done," Magnolia said.

Mrs. Fuller tugged at the strings of her prayer *kapp*. And then she pulled at her neckline as though gasping for air. "I must have done something wrong with him. Perhaps I gave too much attention to the older boys and then when Benjamin came along I gave him too much of my time. I have failed Timothy somewhere, somehow. Otherwise, he wouldn't have done it. It's all my fault."

"You can't blame yourself for what happened. Even if it was the case."

Mary Lou tried to figure out what Magnolia said. It didn't make much sense, but her voice was soothing, so Mary Lou went along with it. "That's true, Ivy. You can't blame yourself."

"That's right, look at the dreadful upbringing Hazel had with her mother and everything."

Mary Lou looked at Magnolia, a little surprised. "I guess that's true. We all know Hazel didn't have the best upbringing with her *vadder*. And then her *mudder* couldn't handle things, but let's not talk about that. Hazel's *Mamm* is doing a lot better now that she's here and living with Hazel and Isaac."

Ivy nodded. "Hazel did grow up with a sensible head on her shoulders, but that's not the case with Timothy, so you can't compare the two. I know you were just trying to make me feel better. Bless you, dear girls."

Mary Lou said, "It's really not as bad as you think. They're a married couple and *Gott* will make a way for them."

"How will it be? Taylor's gone back to her parents. That boy can't even act right in a marriage. Otherwise, she would've stayed with him. He failed marriage."

"They're still very much in love. They're just not together until Timothy sets himself up financially," Magnolia said.

"That girl is not from our world. She is just too different from us, and I don't see that anything will work between them. I don't know what's going to become of Timothy," Ivy Fuller dabbed at her eyes once more.

While Mary Lou rubbed Ivy's arm, Magnolia said, "Timothy is really upset too. You have to understand that."

"You're young, Magnolia. I appreciate you coming here to discuss the matter, but you've still got a great many experiences ahead of you." Ivy shook her head. "And I just don't know what's going to become of him."

"*Jah*, you're right, but he's only young, so he'll find his way."

Ivy shook her head. "I don't think so."

Mary Lou said, "He's come over here to talk to you. Why don't you come out and hear what he has to say?"

"I can't until Obadiah comes home. I don't have the strength to talk to him by myself. He should be home soon." After a moment of silence, Ivy said, "Well, I might be able to go out to talk to him now."

"Do you want us to come with you, or do you want to speak to him alone?" Mary Lou asked.

"Come with me. I don't think we have any secrets. We are a united family."

"We have to make the best of what's happened. We can't turn back the clock and Timothy can't make different choices, and he's done a good thing by marrying Taylor. So there are lots of positives to this situation."

Ivy nodded. "You're right, Mary Lou. You're such a sweet girl." Ivy leaned over and hugged both Mary Lou and Magnolia. *"Denke."* Ivy stood up and then straightened herself up. Then she walked down the stairs with Mary Lou and Magnolia following.

CHAPTER 12

"TIMOTHY, come and talk with us in the kitchen," Mrs. Fuller said as she stood there with Magnolia and Mary Lou behind her.

Timothy looked a little surprised. "Don't you want to wait for *Dat* to come home?"

"That won't be necessary. I'm sure he'll go along with any decisions that I might make."

"Of course." They all sat around one end of the kitchen table.

Timothy cleared his throat. "I've come to ask you if I can come home."

Ivy's eyebrows arched high, causing deep creases in her forehead. "You want to come home and live under this roof?"

"That's right."

"What about Taylor?" Mary Lou asked.

"I'm tired. I'm tired of struggling to try to make things work. I realized that I've been running away from *Gott* and He's the one who can fix up the mistakes I've made and make them right. I am throwing myself on *Gott's* mercy and asking Him to take me back, and I have a strong feeling that if I get my life right and Taylor sees that, she will join me."

"And join the community?" Ivy asked.

"Of course, join the community."

His mother looked at him. "Do you ... Have you talked about this with her?"

"We've had many long conversations about lots of things and about *Gott*. I'm pretty positive she might join us."

Mary Lou listened. 'Pretty positive' that she 'might' didn't sound that positive at all.

"If you want to come back into this *haus* and turn your life over to *Gott*, I'm not going to stand in your way."

"Really?" Timothy couldn't keep the smile from his face. "*Denke, Mamm.*" That meant he no longer had to pay that ridiculously high rent, and the quicker he paid off his debts, the quicker he could create a proper life for his family.

"That's wonderful, Timothy. And would you join

your brothers at the Fullers' Joinery factory again?" Magnolia asked.

"They said when I left they'd take me back. I've got two jobs at the moment, so I would have to see which pays me the most. I have quite a few things I have to pay off."

His mother shook her head. "You've also got debts?"

"I have. It was the cars mostly."

Mrs. Fuller shook her head again. "At least you're trying to turn your life around."

"I am, I have to change something. I realize that. In any case, if anything's gonna change I realize it starts with me. In a way, I wish I'd never gone on *rumspringa*, but then again it's made me grow up."

"And you also wouldn't have met Taylor if you hadn't gone," Magnolia said.

He looked directly at his mother's expression, and he knew that her mother was thinking it would've been a good thing if he had never met Taylor. His mother's opinion would change once she got to know Taylor.

"Would you meet her, *Mamm?* Maybe have her to dinner? Meet your grand *dochder?*"

"One step at a time, Timothy. Let's just get you

back into the community. If you're serious, you'll get baptized."

Timothy gulped. He was put on the spot. He preferred to wait and see how things panned out, but then again, if he was going to make a commitment he had to make a public commitment. "*Jah*, I will get baptized."

"*Gut*. Then you can see the bishop tomorrow and find out when you can begin your instructions."

"I can't see the bishop tomorrow because I'm working two jobs tomorrow."

"When are you figuring on moving back?" Benjamin walked into the kitchen.

"I was hoping I could come on Saturday?"

"*Jah*, Saturday will be fine. I'll help you."

"*Denke*, I don't have much to bring here, but I would appreciate a ride."

TIMOTHY WAS home by ten o'clock that night in time to call Taylor at the usual time.

"My brothers and my family will help us, now that I'll be living back home and …"

"Where are we going to live if you go back? Do you even have a plan?"

She was speaking as though he was a young teenager. He hadn't acted very mature around her, so he couldn't blame her for talking to him in that way. He had to prove himself somehow. "Will you come to the community one day do you think?"

"I don't know much about it, but I believe in God."

"That's a good start." He was pleased she didn't say no.

"Since I met you, I started looking into things about God and Jesus."

"You never said."

"You never asked."

"Will you come to Samuel's wedding on Saturday?"

"I don't think it would be a good idea."

He thought about what a fuss it would create when everyone found out he had a baby. "You're probably right."

CHAPTER 13

MAGNOLIA AND MARY LOU sat in Catherine's parents' house with the other guests while Catherine and Samuel were getting married. In the middle of the ceremony, Mary Lou glanced at Magnolia to see a sullen face. Her face had been sour ever since the couple had stood in front of the bishop. Mary Lou knew she was thinking it should've been she who was marrying Samuel. After the trouble Magnolia had tried to create between the couple, Mary Lou was a little surprised she'd come back to the community so soon, and even more surprised that she thought nothing of attending the wedding.

Magnolia leaned toward her. "Mary Lou, which one is James and which one is Gabe?"

Mary Lou scowled at Magnolia. She knew not to

be talking during the wedding ceremony. "Stop talking," she whispered back.

"Just tell me and I'll stop."

Mary Lou looked behind her. She leaned closer to Magnolia. "I can't see Gabe, but James is sitting down the back, last row second on the left, but don't look now."

"Will you introduce—"

"Quiet. If you'll be quiet and don't say another word, I'll introduce you to the both of them, all right? Can you do that?"

Magnolia smiled and nodded. Over the next several minutes, Magnolia turned around more than once, which greatly annoyed Mary Lou. The third time Magnolia turned around, Mary Lou dug her in the ribs.

"He doesn't know I'm looking at him," Magnolia hissed.

"I'm starting to wish I hadn't told you about him."

Suddenly, the voice of Martin King, one of the ministers who had taken his turn to speak after the bishop, boomed loudly, "Mary Lou, do you have something you'd like to say? Something you'd like to share with everyone?"

Mary Lou's cheeks flushed beet red, and the people in the front rows turned to look at her. *"Nee."*

When he resumed talking, Mary Lou hung her head and was glad Magnolia sat in silence for the rest of the service. It was an embarrassment. It wasn't just a Sunday meeting; she'd just interrupted Catherine and Samuel's wedding. She hoped they'd forgive her. It was a mistake inviting Magnolia to her house. She had only done so in the spirit of forgiveness and fellowship, and now God was using her cousin to test her patience.

WHEN THE SERVICE was over and Magnolia and Mary Lou moved out of the house with the other guests, Magnolia rubbed her arms up down. "It's too cold to have the wedding breakfast outside."

"It's not that cold for so early in the year."

"Introduce one of them to me now, would you?"

Mary Lou looked at Jacob, her husband. All she wanted to do was be with him, but then he would see that Magnolia was annoying her, which would result in him telling her she shouldn't have invited her. He'd been against it, given the recent trouble she'd caused, and now Mary Lou realized she should've listened to him.

Mary Lou suggested, "Why don't you mix a little

bit and talk to the friends that you made last time you were here?"

"I would if I had made any friends last time I was here. Things didn't go that well if you can remember what happened with Catherine. My *mudder* said—"

"I don't need to be told what your mother said. Is she here?"

"*Nee*, but—"

"I know what she said. You've already told me one hundred times since you arrived here."

"Oh, you're cranky today."

What she needed was a few minutes away from her cousin. She felt like she was being strangled. "I'll talk to some different people and when some time has passed, I'll find you and introduce you to some men. Let me just see who's here first, okay?"

Magnolia cocked her head to one side. "You'll fetch me?"

"I will." Mary Lou turned around and saw that there weren't many people gathered around the newly married couple. She walked away from Magnolia and apologized to Catherine and Samuel for what happened during the service.

They were so happy they'd barely noticed the interruption and told her she shouldn't let it trouble her. When more people stepped up to congratulate them, Mary Lou headed off to spend a few moments with Jacob.

He looked up and walked to meet her. "What was that about in there?"

Mary Lou shook her head. "I'm so embarrassed. Magnolia kept talking and I was trying to make her stop."

Jacob chuckled. "You do like to take on projects. First Timothy and now Magnolia."

"I haven't finished with Timothy."

"He's here today. Is that your doing?"

Mary Lou giggled. "It was entirely his idea to come back to live with your parents."

He stared at her. "Hmm."

"It was."

He looked around the crowd. There must've been three hundred people there. "Where's Magnolia?"

"Hopefully mixing with others. I needed a little break from her before I start introducing her to two men I've selected."

He shook his head. "I knew this would happen. Who are the lucky men?"

"Gabe and James."

He stared at her and blinked a couple of times, looking as though he thought them both totally unsuitable. "Aren't they a little old?"

"Nee, not really." They were talking about Magnolia. She wasn't as young as she used to be, and she was no prize. Not that Mary Lou would say that to anyone, but that's what she thought.

He nodded and pulled his mouth to one side, the way he usually did when he disagreed with her. "Let's get something to eat." Together they headed to the food table.

CHAPTER 14

Timothy sat down outside the Millers' house. He'd just watched his next-older brother get married and the whole time he wished it could've been himself and Taylor having the Amish wedding.

He regretted getting married outside the community, but still, his marriage was valid and legal, and it had legitimized Miranda. But where was Taylor? That was the thing that really upset him.

He couldn't concentrate on what the bishop had said and once they were pronounced married, Timothy had to fight back the tears. He hoped … more than that, he prayed that everything would work out and one day he would sit at a wedding with his wife in the same room just like all the other Amish husbands and wives.

He didn't regret his marriage to Taylor even though it meant he could never marry another woman, not even an Amish woman. He didn't want another; he wanted Taylor or nobody. She was the only woman for him and, with their baby, they already had a family. He was missing time already in his baby's life and that was another thing that upset him, just as much as being without Taylor.

He was on a seat under a tree in the Millers' yard when he shut his eyes tightly and silently cried out to God. Part of him was missing; it felt like a gaping wound without the two of them in his life, and he didn't know if that was what God had planned. He opened his eyes when he felt someone nearby. It was Isaac, his oldest brother.

"Can I have a word with you?" Isaac asked, sitting down next to him.

"Of course."

"Now that you're back in the community, have you considered coming to work for us again?"

"I didn't think you'd want me back." He knew he'd only have to ask, but he'd been embarrassed to do so.

"We never wanted you to leave. You're the one who chose to leave when you went on *rumspringa*, remember?"

Timothy adjusted his hat. "Ah, that's right. It all seems like a lifetime ago."

"Well, what do you say?"

The wage from the factory was equivalent to the wage of his day job and he'd much prefer to work with his brothers. "*Jah. Denke,* I'll give notice at my day job tomorrow."

Isaac narrowed his eyes. "Day job?"

"*Jah,* I have a day job and a night job. I need them both, plus more, to pay down my debts."

"Why don't you quit both jobs? You can do over-time with us as well."

"Is that an option?"

Isaac smiled. "It has been for the last few months. We've got orders flooding in."

"Does that mean I'll be able to do a day job and carry through to the evening?"

"Apart from sleeping and eating, we'll give you as much work as you can handle. And extra pay for the extra hours, as usual."

That was a relief to Timothy. It would cut down the traveling time from the day job to the evening job and it would save him bus money. "I'll take it." He put out his hand for Isaac to shake and he shook it.

"Glad to hear it. And, when are we going to meet Taylor?"

"I'm hoping *Mamm* will invite her to dinner."

"Are you waiting for her to suggest it?"

Timothy nodded. "*Jah*."

"Why don't you tell *Mamm* you're planning on inviting her to the next Friday night dinner?"

"You think I should?"

"*Jah*. Suggest it to *Mamm*, and you can even say I thought it was a good idea."

"Okay, *denke*, Isaac."

Isaac slapped him on the shoulder.

"I'm hoping Taylor will come back … I mean, I'm hoping she'll come to the community one day."

"If that's what *Gott* wills then it'll happen."

"I'm hoping that's what He wills and I'm praying about it like crazy."

"I'll help you pray."

"*Denke*, Isaac."

Isaac stood and then headed over to Hazel, who was trying to stop young Abe from darting to and fro. His brother, Levi and his wife, Lucy, were expecting their first at around the same time as Hazel and Isaac were expecting their second. The next generation of the Fuller family was growing and Timothy hoped that one day, Taylor and he would have more children, but first a great many problems had to be resolved.

Working back at the Fuller's joinery factory was a giant step forward, especially if he could do so many hours for the same pay plus the overtime pay. Maybe God had listened to his prayers after all. He headed over to Mary Lou who was helping herself to food with Jacob. "Hi, Mary Lou."

She looked up. "Hello, Timothy. How are things?"

"About the same, but I just got my old job back and I can do overtime."

"Wunderbaar!"

"You've helped me a great deal, Mary Lou, and you've helped Taylor. I want to thank you for that." It came into his mind that Taylor had wanted to name the baby Mary Lou, but he wouldn't share that with his sister-in-law because he was the one who hadn't wanted that to happen.

Mary Lou stepped away from the table with a full plate. "It must be hard for you being here at a wedding when Taylor's not with you."

"It is, but that's just the way it is until she decides to join us."

"Do you want Mary Lou to talk with her again?" Jacob offered as he stood beside Mary Lou.

"*Nee, denke,* she's done enough already. More than

anybody else has done for us." He shook his head thinking about her parents. "There's nothing that can be done now. It's in *Gott's* hands."

Jacob said, "We'll keep you both in our prayers."

"I would appreciate that, the more prayers, the better. Isaac did suggest having Taylor to the family meal on Friday."

"That's a great idea," Mary Lou said.

Timothy chuckled. "It is, but now I have to get *Mamm* to agree with it."

"Have you mentioned it to her?"

"Not yet," he said with a sigh.

"Do you want me to suggest it?" Mary Lou asked.

"Would you?" It would help his mother agree to it if Mary Lou asked her. He was sure of it.

"*Jah,* I think I can make her see that it's a good idea."

"*Denke,* Mary Lou, if you wouldn't mind doing us one more favor."

"Of course. I'm only too happy to help. Just ask me anything that you need." She glanced over at Mrs. Fuller. "As soon as she's by herself, I'll head over to her. I'll work the conversation around to you and how upset you must be feeling today and then I'll suggest that she invites Taylor to the family dinner. After all, she is a Fuller now, one of the family."

"*Jah,* she is," Jacob agreed, as he looked longingly at his plate of food.

"I'll leave you both to eat."

Mary Lou said, "I'll give you a nod when it's all arranged. Will Taylor come if we arrange it?"

Timothy smiled. "I'm certain she will."

CHAPTER 15

Tɪᴍᴏᴛʜʏ ʟᴇꜰᴛ the wedding at the same time as his parents, and at ten o'clock he called Taylor from the phone in the barn. She answered his call sounding like she'd been asleep.

"Did I wake you?" he asked.

"I was waiting for your call and I just drifted off to sleep."

"How do you feel about coming to dinner with the family on Friday night?" He replayed in his mind the bright smile on Mary Lou's face as she gave him the nod that she'd arranged it all with his mother.

There was silence for a moment. "With your whole family?"

"My brothers and their wives, one baby and my mother and father. Also, maybe my sister in law's mother, and a house guest of one of my sisters-in-law. What do you say?"

"Sounds like a lot of people."

"It is."

"Did they invite me?"

"The invitation came from my mother."

There was a moment of silence. "Wow. That's a huge step forward."

"I know."

"When did you say it was?"

"This Friday night."

"Of course I'll come. It'd be rude not to accept. Your mother is reaching out to me. That means a lot."

"Will your parents allow you out of the house?"

Taylor chuckled. "I'm not a prisoner. I can come and go as I please. And now they'll have no choice."

"Why's that?"

"Because I've agreed to some stupid dinner they're having on Thursday night with some man they're trying to match me up with. He's a doctor. I might've mentioned that to you before. They're always going on and on about him."

This was Timothy's worst fear. What if she fell in love with the doctor and she wanted a divorce or an annulment? "You agreed to it? I can't believe it. Your parents are trying to match you with someone else, and you agreed?"

"Calm down. You're such a hothead sometimes. I'm not going to fall in love with anybody when I'm in love with you. You're being crazy."

"I hope not. About the falling in love part, I mean. The crazy part? I'm crazy about you."

"My mother kept on and on about it, so I agreed just to keep her happy. This is perfect now because she won't mind me going on Friday night. In fact, I'll tell her now and if she says anything about it I'll just refuse to show on Thursday. I've got them over a barrel." Taylor giggled.

Timothy wasn't pleased it had to be this way, but as long as she showed up on Friday night that was all he could care about right now. "Shall I collect you at six on Friday?"

"It might be better if I came there by myself."

"Do you think so?"

"I'm sure of it. I'd love to have you come and get us, but my parents would have a fit."

She was probably right. "Okay. How's Miranda?"

"She was a little fussy today."

"That's because she misses me."

"We both miss you very much."

He kept from her the fact that he was arranging

to get baptized into the Amish community. If he left the community after that, he'd be shunned, but he'd been through worse.

"Your brother's wedding was today, wasn't it?" Taylor asked.

"Yeah, Samuel's wedding. He married Catherine. Her other two sisters married two of my older brothers."

"Keep it in the family."

He chuckled. "Yeah, something like that."

"All you Amish seem to be close."

"We are mostly. We're just like one happy family mostly."

"Well, I wouldn't know what that's like."

"Maybe you'll find out one day."

She gave a little giggle. "Maybe."

Timothy sighed. "I wish I was there with both of you right now."

"Me too. I must get some sleep while the baby's asleep. I love you, Timothy. "

"And I love you more, Mrs. Fuller."

She giggled again. "I'll talk to you tomorrow night."

"Bye, love you," he said.

"I love you. You hang up first."

"No, you first," he insisted.

"We'll do one, two, three."

"Okay."

They said together, "One, two, three."

Taylor hung up, but Timothy hung on. He couldn't bear to be the first to hang up. When he finally replaced the phone's receiver, he headed back to the house. It had been a big day, and the light was still on in the kitchen, and light glowed from his parents' bedroom.

He hoped both of his parents had gone to bed. He couldn't face a serious conversation tonight. His mother had agreed to the Friday night dinner with Taylor, and she wasn't one to go back on what she said, but she could certainly have a lot to say about it.

CHAPTER 16

WHEN TIMOTHY WAS BACK in the house, he poked his head around the kitchen doorway and saw Benjamin tucking into a huge sandwich.

"Didn't you eat at the wedding?"

He looked up at Timothy. "I'm a growing boy. I need to eat."

Timothy shook his head. "I don't know where you put everything."

"I heard a rumor that Taylor's coming to dinner Friday night."

Timothy sat down at the table with him. "You heard correctly."

"I'll finally get to speak to this wife of yours."

"It seems so." It played on Timothy's mind that she was having dinner with a single man on

Thursday night. He did his best to push the fearful thoughts away.

"You don't look very happy about it."

"I am. I'm really happy about it. There just seem so many things that stand in our way." He leaned back in the chair and stared at his younger brother. "Have you ever been in love?"

Benjamin nodded. "Several times."

Timothy chuckled. "True love is different. You just love that one person, and nothing and nobody else matters."

In between mouthfuls, Benjamin nodded. "I've been there."

He narrowed his eyes at Benjamin. "You never said anything."

"I feel like that about one girl one week, and then I feel like that about a different one the next week. How do you know when it's real? I'm a bit fearful that I'll marry one *maidel* and like her friend the next week. And then I'll be stuck."

"You'll know when you know."

"Means nothing to me," Benjamin mumbled.

"Maybe give it time and if you like a *maidel* for longer than a week that might be a clue right there."

Benjamin raised his eyebrows and took another

mouthful of his enormous roast beef and lettuce sandwich.

"It's just that I'm worried that her parents are having too much influence on her."

Benjamin swallowed his mouthful. "If it's true love like you say, you've got nothing to worry about."

"I know how I feel, but what if it's different for her?"

"If it's true love, you've got nothing to worry about." Benjamin smirked as he repeated his words.

"But I do worry."

"You know what I've noticed about you lately?"

Timothy was surprised that he'd noticed anything about him at all. "What's that?"

"You're worried all the time."

"Of course I'm worried. I'm completely in love with a woman, we have a child together, and she's not living with me. Do you know how that feels?"

"Nope."

"It feels dreadful." He put his hand over his heart. "It's the worst pain in the world."

"What's stopping you from being together?"

"Money mostly. Her parents have money, I have none, and I have nothing to offer her."

"What do you want to offer her?"

"Stability, a house, a secure future."

"A *haus?* That part is easy. How many brothers have you got?"

"Six."

"Can all of 'em build?"

"*Jah, Dat* taught us all to build things as soon as we could walk. Where are you

going with this?"

"Okay." He placed the last of his sandwich down and dusted off his hands. "You've got brothers and a father with more land than they'll ever use. One of them will allow you to build on their land. Then we'll all pitch in and build it. It shouldn't take that long. And we can fix you a nice kitchen, obviously. Kitchens are what we Fullers do best."

"Yeah, but I can't pay for any of it. I'm already in debt up to my eyeballs."

"We'll all pitch in."

If that suggestion had come from Isaac, he might've thought that was a good idea, but would any of the other brothers agree to it? "They're all still building Samuel and Catherine's house. That's a priority because Samuel doesn't want to live with Catherine's parents forever."

"Nah, not necessarily. He's got a roof over his head and he's living with his *fraa;* even if that is a slight inconvenience for him. Your situation is more urgent."

Timothy nodded. He certainly thought it was. "You think the others will agree?"

"I don't see why not. That's the answer to your problems. You can have a home. I'd say for starters, just have a two bedroom, one bathroom, and then you can add to it as your family increases."

Timothy rubbed his chin. It was starting to sound like a good idea. "If everyone's willing to do this, then I would have a home—a place where we can be a family."

Benjamin nodded. "I'd do it."

"I couldn't ask anyone."

"I'll organize it. You just leave it up to me."

"Leave it up to you? The person who forgot to tell everybody I was married?"

Benjamin dusted off his hands and pushed the empty plate to the center of the table. "That was different. There was nothing to organize. I like organizing things."

"Okay, I'll leave it up to you and your organizational skills."

Benjamin tapped his chin. "There is a nice piece of land right here on this property. It's raised up slightly and it has a *wunderbaar* view. I had it in the back of my mind for myself because I don't want to stay living here forever, but it would be perfect. It's down by the south pasture. I'll show you tomorrow morning on our way to work."

"*Denke,* Benjamin, I appreciate all this. But it's all dependent on Taylor wanting to join us. And I fear that there's not much chance of that."

"'I fear this, I fear that.' And look at that sad face. You said it's true love. She loves you, you've got a child together, and she's already been to one or two community weddings."

Timothy nodded.

"You have to see that there are no problems. Major problems are left to *Gott* and He works everything out, but you have to trust Him. Otherwise, your prayers won't work."

"What do you mean?"

"Ever heard of faith?"

Timothy sat still and didn't utter a word. Benjamin, his little brother, was right. Worrying was not trusting, and not trusting was having no faith. He had to learn to have faith in God.

Benjamin stood and pushed in his chair.

Timothy remained seated. "We'll leave for work early so you can show me this prized piece of land."

"Okay." Benjamin washed and rinsed off his plate and left it on the rack to dry.

"Are you heading to bed now?" Timothy asked.

"Hmm, I was, but now I feel like another sandwich. Want one?"

Timothy chuckled and stood up. *"Nee denke."* He headed to his bedroom where he would pray, try to be less fearful, and ask for stronger faith.

CHAPTER 17

THROUGHOUT THURSDAY, Timothy was dreadfully worried that Taylor might become interested in the doctor that she and her parents were entertaining that night. Then he remembered about faith. He stopped being fearful and started his process of trusting. Every time fear tried to creep in he said to himself, "*Gott* will provide."

When he called Taylor that night at the usual time, she didn't answer. His struggles with faith began all over again. "*Gott* will provide," he whispered. It crossed his mind to go to Taylor's parents' house but, after he thought it over, he realized it would be a big mistake. Just as he was about to pick up the phone's receiver and dial again, the phone rang. "Taylor?"

"Ya, it's me."

"I was a little worried. How did it go?"

"It's still going. Now our guest is in the library with my father, drinking brandy."

"That doesn't sound good."

"If my parents like him so much they can marry him."

Timothy chuckled.

"All I want to do is go to bed. Miranda went to sleep two hours ago."

"Well, just say good night to him and go to bed."

"I wish I could. That would be considered very rude."

"And?"

Taylor giggled. "You're right. I needn't care what any of them think. I am trying to keep on my parents' good side as much as possible, though, because I am living under their roof."

"Hopefully not for long."

Timothy heard Taylor's mother in the background. "Taylor, are you there?"

"I'm coming in a minute, Mom." She waited a moment, and then said, "That's Mom. I can't even be away for two minutes. I'll just tell them I'm tired and need to go to bed. Hopefully, they'll understand."

"They should. You're a new mother after all. And

a doctor surely ought to realize that you need to get your sleep."

"I'll do it. Good night, Timothy."

"Good night."

She quickly hung up. There was no back and forth banter over who was going to hang up first like there usually was, thanks to her mother. Timothy hung up the receiver and made his way out of the darkened barn pleased Taylor wasn't falling in love with the doctor. He gave a little chuckle as he thought how silly he'd been to think it might be a possibility. They were both equally in love with each other. He hoped that tomorrow night she would see she could fit in well with his family. He only hoped his mother would be nice to her because his mother could be a little cold sometimes. Surely, the baby would soften her heart.

ON FRIDAY NIGHT, Timothy made sure he was home in plenty of time and now he waited on the porch for Taylor. His brothers and sisters arrived, and he kept waiting. Then Taylor arrived in a large black car driven by the same driver who'd taken them to Florida to get married.

He walked out and opened the door for Taylor, and gave a quick nod to the driver. She stepped out, and Timothy unbuckled the baby from the car seat. "Look how big she is now." He gently touched her soft cheek with the back of his hand and his heart swelled with love as he snuggled her in against his chest.

"You saw her only a few days ago."

"She's grown so much since then. Nearly doubled in size."

A soft giggle sounded from Taylor's lips. "She's only put on a little weight. Stop exaggerating."

As he held the baby in his arms, they walked to the house side-by-side.

"I'm a little nervous," she admitted.

"There's no need to be."

"Easy for you to say."

When they reached the front door, Timothy pushed it open with his foot and allowed Taylor to walk through first. They were both faced with the whole family standing in a semicircle and staring at Taylor and Miranda and him.

CHAPTER 18

TIMOTHY GULPED, hoping Taylor wouldn't feel awful with all these strangers gawking at her. Even though she'd been to Mary Lou and Jacob's wedding, formal introductions were now warranted. "Everyone, this is Taylor, and this is Miranda." Nobody said a word, and then Timothy went from left to right introducing his family to Taylor.

The first friendly step forward toward Taylor was from Mrs. Fuller. "Welcome to our home, Taylor. Might I have a hold of the baby?"

"Of course, you can. She's your granddaughter."

Timothy passed the baby over to his mother and from the look on his mother's face, he knew that everything would be all right.

His mother hugged the baby. "How precious she is. Little ... little Miranda."

His sisters-in-law gathered around and admired the baby while Mary Lou talked to a somewhat relieved-looking Taylor. After a few minutes, Mr. Fuller ushered everybody away from the door and into the living room.

As they walked into the living room, Timothy whispered to Taylor, "Sorry about that. It was a bit awkward."

"It's okay. They're friendly."

Mrs. Fuller gave the baby to Adeline, one of her daughters-in-law, and then Hazel and Mrs. Fuller went into the kitchen to finish off the preparation of the meal. Everybody was taken with little Miranda, especially when she opened her eyes from her nap. Then Adeline offered Mr. Fuller a turn holding the baby. He quickly accepted, a smile lighting his eyes.

Soon everybody was sitting around the extra-long dining table. They all said their silent prayers of thanks and then started passing the food and serving themselves.

"This food is delicious, Mrs. Fuller," Taylor said.

"You don't need to call me Mrs. Fuller, just call me Ivy."

"All right, Ivy, thank you."

Timothy was a little disappointed that his mother didn't say to call her *Mamm,* but then he realized all of his brothers' wives called her Ivy. After a slightly awkward beginning, everyone started talking.

When the dinner was over, Timothy and Taylor stayed at the table with his mother and father while the rest of the family moved back to the living room.

"I'm so pleased you came tonight, Taylor."

"Thank you for inviting me, Mrs. Fuller...um, I mean, Ivy."

Timothy looked at his father and was happy to see him smiling. He wasn't much of a talker unless someone got him talking about building or wood.

"I do hope you can come again soon, Taylor," his mother said a short time later.

"I'd like to."

The polite conversation between Taylor and his mother continued for several minutes until Taylor said, "I should go. It's getting late and Miranda is due for a feeding soon."

After Taylor said goodbye to everyone, Timothy walked outside with his wife and child.

"Shall I call your driver?"

"Yes please." She told him the number.

"I'll never remember that. Come with me." Together they walked to the barn and Timothy switched on the gas lantern by the door. "What did you think of them all?"

"They're all really lovely. Even your mother's nice and your father's quite funny once he starts to talk. And all your brothers are so handsome."

"But not as handsome as me, right?"

"Of course, they aren't," she said with a smile. "No one is as handsome as you. I'll dial, you take the baby." She called the driver and then hung up. "He'll be about twenty minutes to half an hour."

"Shall we wait in here? It's too cold for the baby out there."

They could've gone back inside the house, but he wanted to be alone with Taylor.

"We can wait here out of the wind, that's a good idea. She should be fine; she's wrapped snugly."

"I miss you and Miranda. It's not right that we're not living together."

"I know, but where would we live? I can't go back to that apartment. I'd go mad. I feel so isolated there and it's dark and damp, and cramped."

"I know, but I didn't say I wouldn't be impatient and I didn't say that it was going to be easy."

"It's very hard. I don't want to live with my parents. All I want is to be out of their way. They want to control me."

128

He nodded.

She looked down at his clothing. "I notice you're wearing Amish clothing. What's going on with that?"

"I came back here to live."

"Yeah, but just to save money, right?"

He looked down; he had hoped he could break it to her in a gentler manner. "I came back because I need to get my life right with God."

He could see the hurt and disbelief in her eyes, when she said, "Where does that leave Miranda and me?"

"You're part of my life."

"It doesn't seem like that if you just make decisions by yourself. Does that mean I have to join and is that the only way we can be together?"

"Something like that."

She raised her voice. "Timothy, why can't you grow up?"

His mouth opened wide and he stared at her. "I'm trying to be the best man I can be for all of us."

"You're selfish. You can't just make a big lifetime decision like that and expect me to join your community, a community that I know next to nothing about."

"You do know some things about it. You asked

questions and I answered them, and you've even gone to—"

"You didn't tell me much. All I really know is you drive buggies and wear certain clothing and have these rules that you live by. I've looked on the Internet and I kind of understand it, but I don't know if I can leave my world to live in this one. This wasn't the plan, Timothy. That wasn't *our* plan. And you went ahead like this without me."

"I'm trying to do what's right for all three of us."

"You can't make these decisions without consulting me."

"I'm the head of the household."

She narrowed her eyes at him. "Does that mean you're a dictator? Because that won't work, not with me." She took her cell phone out of her bag and called someone. Timothy waited and looked on in silence. "How far away are you?" Timothy knew she was talking to the driver. "Would you please hurry even if you have to speed?" She ended the call.

"Are you that anxious to get away from me that you'd have your driver speed?"

"Yes, because I'm cranky with you."

This was the first real argument they'd ever had, and Timothy feared it would be their last. "I don't know what to say."

"Don't say anything," she snapped.

Timothy walked closer to her and she walked out of the barn. "Things will work out because we're in love with each other."

"This is the real world, Timothy. Grow up."

Her words hurt him. He was trying to make adult decisions, and to hear her keep telling him to grow up made him feel so much worse. He stared at her as she gazed down at the road waiting for the driver. His worst fear would be that she would see more of that doctor her parents liked. "We shouldn't leave each other in anger."

"You leave me no choice." She hugged the baby to herself.

"I'm sorry I didn't discuss it with you, Taylor."

"Sorry doesn't matter because you've already done it and it's too late."

"That won't matter if you join the community."

"I join? Why should I?" she shrieked. "This is nothing like we planned. I had a whole future ahead of me until I met you. I was going to be a research scientist and you ended all that for me."

He glanced over at the house hoping no one could hear them. "Keep your voice down."

"I don't care who hears us. You're selfish. Just plain selfish. You have Miranda and me to consider and yet you just go ahead and make a huge decision without consulting me."

"It's a little hard to talk with you at any length when you're living with your parents, and I can't even visit you. All I can do is call you at ten each night and by that time you're tired and half asleep. That's no way for us to live as husband and wife, Taylor."

"Maybe we should just forget the whole thing." She walked away further down the drive.

"No, wait."

She swung around. "What am I waiting for, Timothy? Am I waiting for you to grow up?"

There those words were again. Maybe she was right. Maybe he was too immature to handle a wife and a baby. Evidently, she thought he was.

Headlights appeared at the end of the road, and Timothy wondered if things were over.

She met the car halfway down the driveway, and in no time the car was gone.

Timothy didn't want to go inside and face everybody if they'd heard the raised voices. After Taylor and Miranda had left, he waited in the darkened barn and watched his brothers and their wives go home.

All he could think to do was wait in the barn, give Taylor enough time to get home and then call her. He had to say sorry again. Taylor was right. Him going back to the community for good hadn't been in their plans. He had to ask her for forgiveness and together they would decide where to go from there.

After waiting a good amount of time, he dialed her number and there was no answer. He called her again and the ring tone was cut off as though she'd ended the call. He waited until the last of the visitors had left, and then walked into the darkened house and went up to his bedroom to try to get some sleep.

CHAPTER 19

TAYLOR OPENED her bedroom door and placed her sleeping baby down in the crib. Her parents still hadn't reopened her line of credit on her credit card, but they'd given her plenty of money to shop for the baby. They'd had a room repainted for Miranda and she had a small crib covered with white lace and lined with a silky-soft pink fabric. Another crib was waiting for when she grew bigger. Evidently, her parents were under the impression she'd be there for a while.

Taylor was still fuming-angry with Timothy. He had this outdated idea that he had to be the man, the boss, but then again, the Amish were probably all like that and that was something of which she did not approve, not one little bit. To her, marriage partners were a team.

She took her cell phone out of her bag and placed it on the bed and then it rang. She looked down and recognized the number as coming from Timothy's parents' house. She was so angry, she couldn't even bring herself to speak with him.

There was nothing she could say to him. Nothing polite anyway. When the phone timed out and then rang again, she clicked the button on the side to turn off her phone.

She changed into her nightie, wondering all the while if she should end things between herself and Timothy. She had hoped they'd have a happy ending, but now with him back in the Amish community, it was a slap in the face to her and a sign of what their future would be like.

If she were a different kind of person, she'd follow him wherever he went, but she was who she was and she had Miranda to consider. It irritated her that he was trying to pressure her to join the community by going back there. She wasn't going to follow his lead. Timothy had chosen the wrong way to go about things. Had he discussed it with her like a normal human being, then things might've been different. A gentle knock sounded on her bedroom door. "Yes?"

"It's me." It was the voice of her mother.

"What is it?"

"Are you all right?"

"Yes, why wouldn't I be?" Taylor cringed when she heard the rude words come out of her mouth. She didn't mean to be so hostile with her mother, but everybody was annoying her all the time.

"You came home upset. Did that man do something to upset you?"

"That man? You mean Miranda's father, that man?"

"Yes."

"I'm fine, Mother. Thanks for asking, but I just want to be alone."

"Suit yourself. Don't say I didn't ask."

Why was Timothy's life so complicated? For the first time in months, she doubted that Timothy and she could make things work. Perhaps divorce was the only answer for both their sakes. She'd go back to her original plan of never marrying; only she'd be a divorced woman and a single mother. She'd throw herself back into her studies. All Timothy had done was complicate her life. One good thing out of their brief relationship was Miranda, and that was one thing Taylor did not regret in the least.

THE NEXT MORNING, Timothy jumped out of bed and got ready for work. He'd had a sleepless night of tossing and turning. He and Benjamin drove to work by themselves as their semi-retired father had planned to come in later that day. Mr. Fuller liked to keep an eye on the running of the business much to the annoyance Isaac, the oldest son, who was now in charge.

As soon as Timothy arrived at work, he dialed Mary Lou's number hoping she would answer.

"Hello."

"Hi, Mary Lou, it's Timothy."

"Hi, Timothy, what's up?"

"Well, you might have guessed things didn't go too well last night with Taylor and me."

"Mmm, I heard a bit of an argument. What happened?"

He took a deep breath. "I've made a mess of things. She said I should've discussed it with her about coming back to the community."

"Oh, I see."

"Needless to say, she's furious with me. I can see what she means. We're married and should make these decisions together and I just went ahead and made the decision and didn't tell her about it."

"I know what you mean. I tend to do things like that myself sometimes, too."

"You do?"

"That's right," Mary Lou said.

He had no time for idle chit-chat, so he told her about what Benjamin suggested about a house, and after that, he kept to the point. "So how do I get myself out of this mess?"

"Let me think things over."

"*Denke,* Mary Lou. Umm. How long do you think that will take?"

"Why don't I bring lunch in for the two of us and then we can talk things over and formulate a plan?"

"What, today?"

"*Jah.*"

"You're the best, Mary Lou. Today would be great."

"Just tell me, how were things left between the two of you?"

He blew out a deep breath. He didn't even want to think about how dreadful their argument was.

"She didn't pick up when I called her twice last night."

"Okay, leave it with me and I'll think about it. I'll make some sandwiches, will that be okay, or would you prefer something hot?"

"I'm so upset. I don't think I can even eat anything. I didn't have any breakfast, so maybe I'll be hungry by lunchtime. Don't go to any trouble, though. Sandwiches are easier."

"You must eat, you must keep your strength up."

"I know, I know. I'll try to eat at lunchtime."

"I'll see you then." Mary Lou hung up the phone.

For the next few hours, Timothy threw himself into work. He was glad that this sort of work demanded full mental focus. The next thing he knew, Hazel was tapping him on the shoulder telling him Mary Lou was waiting for him in the lunchroom. Hazel, Isaac's wife, did the company's bookwork part-time.

Timothy headed to meet Mary Lou, pleased with himself for putting everything out of his mind for at least a little while.

He walked in to see Mary Lou arranging sandwiches. She looked up when he walked in. "Ah, there you are. I've got a good variety of sandwiches and

I've made us some nice *kaffe*." She tapped the top of her thermos.

"*Denke*. I love your *kaffe*." She made it from scratch and ground her own beans. He sat down in front of her, picked a sandwich from the pile and put it on his plate.

She looked at him surprised. "Aren't you going to wash your hands?"

"Oh, *jah*." He jumped up, washed his hands in the sink and dried them on a paper towel. Mary Lou was starting to remind him of his mother. He sat back down. "The thing I'm worried about, and this is something I didn't tell you on the phone, is that there's a doctor that Taylor's parents are trying to match her with. They've had him to their house and everything. She's an *Englischer*, so she'll think nothing of divorcing me."

"You're exaggerating. We aren't the only ones who think twice about divorce."

"I didn't know that." He picked up his sandwich and took a bite. It was chicken and something creamy like mayonnaise, with chopped celery, onion and carrots.

"It's true. Some people outside the community have very much the same views as ours."

"I doubt that's true of Taylor."

"I wouldn't say so. I think she's a lovely girl and she's in love with you. Maybe just give her a few days and things will blow over. Give it a little time."

"Do you think so?" He hoped this wasn't the grand plan she'd come up with—do nothing. He didn't like the sound of that at all.

"I do. Just wait and see."

Timothy smiled to be polite and bit into his sandwich. When he finished his mouthful, he said, "I can't wait and do nothing. I just can't. You said something about devising a plan."

Mary Lou breathed out heavily. "Sometimes, doing nothing IS doing something."

His heart sank. He was a doer, not someone who could wait around. He'd never been patient. "And, if that doesn't work?"

"We go ahead and build that *haus*. The *haus* on your parents' land just like Benjamin said."

That sounded better to him. "I haven't even talked to *Mamm* and *Dat* about it."

"How about you leave that to me?"

"Are you saying that I build the *haus* hoping she'll forgive me and join the community?"

"*Jah.*"

"And what if that doesn't work?"

"Then you'll have a *haus* to live in and somewhere to bring the *boppli* when she visits."

He put his hand to his head. "What a dreadful thought. I don't want my *dochder* to visit me. I want her to live with me and Taylor."

"Hold the vision of what you want in your head. I'll talk to your *mudder*. I'll go there when I finish my sandwich and tell her what we've discussed."

"Don't be disappointed if she doesn't agree." He had faith in Mary Lou. She'd gotten his mother to agree to Taylor coming for dinner.

"Why wouldn't she?"

"She's so upset with me."

"You've come back to the community, haven't you?"

"*Jah.*"

"Then you're like the prodigal son and I'll remind her of that."

Timothy chuckled. "*Denke,* Mary Lou. I know I've been a total pain. You're the only person who could put up with me. And the only person I can trust."

Mary Lou smiled and then took a small bite of her large sandwich.

CHAPTER 20

WHEN TIMOTHY WENT BACK to work, Mary Lou packed up the remainder of the sandwiches and poured the remainder of the coffee down the sink.

Isaac poked his head into the lunchroom. "Who were you having lunch with, Mary Lou?"

"I've just had lunch with Timothy," she said just as Jacob walked into the room.

"This is the first I've heard of it."

"We arranged it this morning. It was a last-minute thing. You'd already left for work."

"Hmm."

Isaac chuckled and walked on, and Mary Lou leaned forward and whispered to Jacob, "He's having problems with Taylor and I'm helping him sort them out."

"And exactly how are you doing that?"

"I'll tell you tonight. I'm on my way to your mother's, and I'll talk with her. There is an idea going around, and I'm going to ask Ivy what she thinks of it."

He nodded. "Thanks for taking such an interest in my *bruder* and his problems." He pulled her toward him and gave her a small kiss on the cheek which made her giggle.

She pulled away and then leaned in to give him a quick kiss in return. "I'll see you tonight."

She looped her basket with the lunch items in it over her arm and continued to the buggy feeling happy that she had a husband like Jacob. God had truly blessed her, and she wanted the same for Timothy and Taylor.

HALF AN HOUR LATER, she knocked on the door at the Fuller home.

"Mary Lou, come in." When Mary Lou was inside, Mrs. Fuller said, "Are you here to talk about the dinner last night?"

"Not really. Um … Do we need to talk about it?"

Mrs. Fuller chuckled. "Not really, but I did hear a bit of a lover's spat, and I know you did too. Come to the kitchen and I'll fix us something to eat. It must be time for the midday meal about now."

"Not for me. I had sandwiches and *kaffe* not too long ago. I couldn't possibly fit anything else in. I'll keep you company, though."

When Mrs. Fuller sat down with a plate of reheated meatloaf, she looked across at Mary Lou. "You look like you're worried about something. What is it?"

"I've come up with an idea. Well, it wasn't my idea. It's something Benjamin mentioned to Timothy. He thought it might be a possibility."

Mrs. Fuller raised her eyebrows. "Go on."

"Timothy and Taylor are married now and have a *boppli* together, and so to attract Taylor to the community, Timothy feels he must have something to offer her."

Mrs. Fuller blinked rapidly. "A dowry?"

"*Nee*, a *haus*."

Mrs. Fuller leaned back in her chair. "The last time I heard, Timothy was in debt and that was yesterday, so how can he get a *haus*?"

Mary Lou swallowed hard. "He's in a bit of debt, actually not a terrible amount now that he's freed from paying the apartment rent, but Benjamin had this idea ..."

She scoffed. "Benjamin had an idea?"

"I believe it is a good one. I know he's got his head in the clouds much of the time, but I don't think he's a man who should be underestimated. Sometimes really great ideas come from such minds."

"Quite right, Mary Lou. Continue."

"The brothers could get together and pay for the materials and build Timothy a house."

"That's an excellent idea, but where would he get the land?"

"Well... I've heard that there's a nice piece of land on the eastern side of your property. It's on a little hill near the south pasture in a large flat area that has a nice view. I don't really know where it is, but Benjamin believes it would be the best place to build."

"On our land, is it?"

"*Jah.*"

"If Obadiah doesn't have any plans for it, I'm sure he won't mind. Are you organizing all this, Mary Lou?"

Mary Lou rubbed the side of her face. It seemed like she was already pretty much doing that. "Yeah, I could, with Benjamin, maybe, since it's his idea. Timothy has so much on his mind. That is, if you and Obadiah are agreeable. You'll have to find out from Benjamin exactly where the land is."

"I'll talk to Obadiah tonight. And I like the idea, and I hope things work out well. Taylor's a nice girl."

Mary Lou was relieved. "I'm so glad you like her."

"She's quiet and shy, and she seems to be a good mother."

"She is. She's very devoted."

Ivy leaned forward. "What was that quarrel about last night?"

"I'm not sure." That wasn't entirely true. Mary Lou knew the reason, but Mrs. Fuller would get the wrong idea altogether if she found out Taylor was upset about Timothy coming back.

"I'll find out from Benjamin where this place is. I'll call you tomorrow, how does that sound?"

"That sounds good. Very good."

"*Denke,* Mary Lou."

CHAPTER 21

THE NEXT MORNING, Mary Lou was in the barn reaching for the phone and it rang, causing her to jump. "Hello?"

"Hi, it's Timothy."

"Oh, Timothy. I was just about to call your work to speak with you. Do you have news?"

"I have very good news. My *vadder* agreed to give me the land, or I should say, give me and Taylor the land."

"Excellent. Have you told Taylor yet?"

"I don't want to talk to her about anything until it's all done. I want it to be a surprise."

Mary Lou hoped that was a good idea, but with Taylor's parents against Timothy, maybe he would be better off telling her sooner. "Have you spoken to her since your disagreement the other night?"

"I haven't and as far as I know, she hasn't tried to call me."

"It is a little hard to call you since she'd have to call the phone in your barn and there isn't always someone in earshot of the barn from inside your *haus*. It's a distance away."

"It sounds like you think I should tell her."

"It would be nice to keep it a secret, but on the other hand, I think she would like to know you're working toward something for your family."

"*Jah,* but think what a lovely surprise she'll get when it's all done and she can see the finished product."

"Okay. How are we going to do this? Your *mudder* seems to think that I'm organizing it."

Timothy chuckled. "That's what she told me."

"I kind of said I was. Why don't Jacob and I host a family meeting about it on Saturday at midday at our place? I can organize everything as much as I can, with Jacob's help, of course. I don't know one thing about building and construction."

"I don't know how I can ever repay you for everything you've done, Mary Lou."

Mary Lou chuckled. "You can repay me by being

as happy as I am, Timothy. And you can stop thanking me. It makes me feel embarrassed."

"I'll try."

"Can you spread the word amongst your brothers for midday on Saturday?"

"I surely will. I can't wait to get started."

Mary Lou replaced the phone's receiver, glad she was being useful. God had not chosen to bless her with children yet, so she had time on her hands. She no longer worked at the café where she'd worked for years before her marriage; she wanted to be a home-maker and Jacob had said that they didn't need the money.

Saturday rolled around, and Mr. Fuller and all the Fuller boys were in Jacob and Mary Lou's house.

Mary Lou stood up. "We all know why we're here?"

"*Jah,*" Benjamin said, half standing. "We're going to build a house for me."

His brothers laughed.

"Nice try. A house for Timothy, thanks to your great idea," Mary Lou said. "Denke, you can sit back down now, Benjamin."

His brothers laughed at him.

"That's right," he said as he sat.

"And how long would it take?" Mary Lou asked, looking at all the eager faces.

Mr. Fuller said, "We could get the basic structure done over one weekend. If it's a small *haus.*"

"I'd only need one bedroom, or even just one room," Timothy said.

Isaac said, "We'll make it a two bedroom with a big living area, a nice eat-in kitchen big enough for company, and a bathroom. We can put up a barn later."

"I appreciate this, everybody. I'll repay you all every cent."

"*Nee,* you won't," Mr. Fuller said. "We're doing this to give you a good start, Timothy. No one wants to be paid back."

Everyone murmured their agreement.

"Does that mean we're starting next weekend?" Mary Lou asked.

"Weather permitting, *jah,*" Mr. Fuller said.

When they started talking about what materials they'd need, Mary Lou sat down to take notes as Jacob stood to take over directing the discussion.

. . .

AFTER EVERYONE LEFT, Magnolia came out of her room and sat down at the kitchen table while Mary Lou was trying to make sense of her notes. Jacob spoke so fast she'd had to scribble to catch the important things he said.

"I see you've been distracted by other things, Mary Lou." Magnolia sat down.

"Oh, I have been a little. You see, we're …"

"*Jah*, I heard it all. And now I know why you haven't bothered to find me a husband. Do you think I'm so ugly that no one would be a match?"

"*Nee*, not at all."

"I'm going home tomorrow."

"*Nee*, we haven't even—"

"I know you can't do two things at once. I'm not angry with you or anything. I just think it's best that you call me when Timothy's house is done and when you've got time to help me."

"I can do it at the same time."

Magnolia shook her head. "If you could've you would've. *Dat's* still laid up, so I've decided to go home and spend time with him. Call me when you're ready and I'll come back."

Mary Lou looked down at her notes, saddened that she'd let Magnolia down. Maybe things were better that way. She looked up at Magnolia. "You will come back?"

"*Jah,* when you get yourself organized. I don't want to have to nag you to find a man for me. Do it and then call me to come and meet him. Or them, if you find more than one prospect. Deal?" Magnolia reached out her hand and Mary Lou smiled and shook it.

This time Magnolia was leaving the community on more pleasant terms. Mary Lou was at least happy about that.

CHAPTER 22

WHEN TAYLOR WOKE, she picked up her cell phone and scrolled through the missed calls. There was nothing there from Timothy. He hadn't called her, and it seemed like it had been weeks. It was time for her baby's check-up at the doctor and more than anything she would've liked Timothy to go with her.

She knew decisions had to be made at this visit regarding immunization. She didn't want to make those decisions alone. She had read some articles on the Internet very much against immunization, even though almost everyone had once been very much for the procedure.

Taylor didn't know what to do and she didn't know if the Amish were for or against such things.

Pride stopped her from calling Timothy, and she guessed he was feeling the same way. Maybe he had given up on the struggle to make their relationship work. Was it too daunting for him to be able to repay all his debts and offer them a reasonable life?

When she heard her baby making noises, she headed to the adjoining room. Before she picked up Miranda, she stared at her for a moment. Her bow-shaped mouth was perfect as were her tiny eyelashes and minute fingernails. All Taylor wanted to give her was a decent life and how could she do that if she went back with Timothy? She'd tried that and it had been a daily grind. She picked her daughter up and held her close.

The only thing she knew to do was stay with her parents and continue her studies. The last thing she wanted to do was live off her parents, but there was no other choice since they'd cut off her trust fund money. She couldn't survive in that dingy apartment of Timothy's. With his debts draining all the money, he barely brought in enough money for food. She wanted the best for her baby, and with Timothy, there would be continual struggle. Things would be different when she got her trust fund money at twenty-five, but Timothy already said he wanted to be the provider. So, there would be problems even then. And that was too far away to think about.

Had she known the situation she would've found herself in she would've been better prepared. But Timothy had burst into her life like an afternoon storm on a summer's day, and she had been unprepared for his love or her response to it.

She changed Miranda's diaper while wondering what to do. She badly wanted to talk to Timothy and hear his voice again. She reminded herself he'd be at work, and she didn't have his work number. It wouldn't take much to find it, though. After she'd changed Miranda, she took her back to her room to feed her.

It annoyed her that Timothy hadn't called her and if he wasn't man enough to call, why should she bother calling him? Didn't he want to see their child, at least? It had been weeks since he'd seen her. He hadn't seen his baby's first smile nor had he seen how big she had grown. Her husband was turning into a disappointment in more ways than one.

LATER THAT DAY, Taylor sat in front of the doctor with her baby in her arms.

"Your baby is due for immunizations today. And

there are a few of them." The doctor turned around to begin the preparations for the immunizations without even asking if she wanted them given.

"No, wait. I'm a bit concerned about the whole thing."

He frowned at her like no one had ever questioned him. "What do you mean?"

"I just would rather talk to her father first before she gets any immunization."

His gray eyebrows drew together. "Is your husband a doctor?"

"No, but it's a decision we should make together. I know everyone doesn't immunize and I don't know if my baby's father would like it done or not and I'm still not sure how I feel about it. He has certain religious beliefs."

"I see. Do you want to call him now? You can use my phone?"

"Oh no, he's away and not contactable."

The doctor looked a little put-out. "We recommend that this first set is given at eight weeks, so talk to him and then come back as soon as possible. You won't need a separate appointment, just call and tell the receptionist when you're coming."

"Yes, I'll do that."

"Very well." He proceeded to examine the baby.

Taylor found out that Miranda was progressing normally and in excellent health. Before she left the doctor's office, he said, "We do have immunizations for a reason you know."

Taylor nodded. "I know. I'll talk to him as soon as I can about them."

"Very good."

Taylor put her baby back in the stroller and headed out of the clinic. She was supposed to call the driver when she was ready to go home, but she was so upset and stressed that she needed some alone time. She battled the heavy glass doors before realizing she could just hit the automatic-opener button and found herself and Miranda on the sidewalk. After a ten-minute walk, she found a park. There she sat under a tree and closed her eyes to pray.

She'd gone to Sunday school as a girl and had believed in God until she had studied science at college. That made her doubt what the Bible said. Upon recent Internet investigation, she had come to understand that there were definite possibilities that the bible supported recent scientific theories. Archaeologists had unearthed biblical places long thought to be fictional. It was a powerful possibility that the bible was real, and if the bible was real, that had to mean that God was real. Taylor wanted to make her life right with God, for her sake and Miranda's.

She prayed that God would somehow make a way for her family to be complete. She didn't want a man like her parents wanted for her, a man only concerned with how he was regarded by people. Taylor wanted a man with old-fashioned principles who would always love her no matter what. At that moment, she regretted moving out of the apartment, knowing that was all Timothy could afford. He was a good and decent man, and he'd been working at two jobs and doing his best, and she knew she'd been 'spoiled' by growing up with wealthy and snobbish parents.

In a flash, she realized how bad she'd made him feel over everything, especially by telling him to 'grow up'. They'd had a roof over their heads, running water, food ... And they'd been together—a family. That was much better than living in her parents' house where there was little love and no Timothy.

She ended her prayers. "God, I just want to be back with Timothy." She wondered about joining the Amish community. It was something she was closer to prepared to do and, the more she'd thought about it over the past weeks, the more plausible the whole thing seemed. The only thing that now stood in her way was that Timothy wasn't contacting her. Had she ruined everything?

She decided that tonight at the usual ten o'clock time she would call him and swallow her pride. She owed him that much.

MIRANDA WAS asleep when Taylor's cell phone read 10:00. She pressed in Timothy's number and hoped he'd be there in the barn. When Timothy answered, her heart nearly pumped out of her chest and she could hardly breathe for an instant. "Timothy." Her voice came out a little shaky.

"I was praying it would be you."

"You haven't called me," she said.

"I was about to."

She didn't know if she could believe him. "Really?"

"I was."

"Just now?"

"That's right. That's why I was right by the phone. I know we haven't talked since the argument weeks ago, but I was just about to call and leave a message on your phone asking you to meet with me tomorrow. I have a surprise I've been working on."

She was pleased he hadn't forgotten her. "A surprise for me?"

"Yes."

"Oh. I hate not knowing things. Tell me now?"

"No. This is something that you must see with your eyes."

She giggled, glad things could be back the way they were. "I can't wait."

"Me either."

"What time do you want me to get there?"

"Ten in the morning. Make sure you bring Miranda."

"Of course, I will. She's always with me."

"I've missed you so much."

"I've missed you, too. We should never fight again," she said, trying not to cry.

"I was in the wrong. I should never have come back here without discussing it with you."

"No, Timothy. I was in the wrong. I should've stayed with you in the apartment and then you wouldn't have had to go back home."

"Let's talk more about it tomorrow. There are so many things I want to tell you face to face, and I don't want to be tempted to say them over the phone. I'm looking forward to seeing you."

"Me too."

"Goodnight, Taylor."

"Night, Timothy."

Timothy waited until Taylor ended the call before he set the receiver down. His body flooded with happiness and light. Taylor was coming back to him; he could feel it. She'd surely be happy with their new home, he hoped.

CHAPTER 23

THE NEXT DAY, Timothy was waiting for Taylor with his buggy hitched and ready. When the car pulled up, he realized he'd never in his life been more excited to see anyone. He walked over to the car and helped unbuckle Miranda from her car seat so Taylor could more easily lift her out. He then grabbed the bag of spare diapers and other baby stuff and closed the door.

"I can't believe how big she's gotten. I hope she didn't forget me."

"I'm sure she didn't." Taylor and Timothy stepped away from the car as it drove away.

Timothy gave Taylor a quick kiss on the cheek. "Are you ready?"

"For the surprise?"

"Yes."

"I can't wait." Her eyes traveled to the buggy. "Are we going in that?"

"We are."

"That's a first for me, kind of exciting."

They drove half a mile down the road so he could approach the land from a different angle. He turned off and drove along the farm lane and then down the clear path to his little cottage. He hoped she would approve and go inside to see how lovely it looked. As nervous as he was, he tried his best to remain upbeat and confident.

"Since we've been apart, I've been thinking about a lot of different things," Taylor said.

He glanced over at her. "Like what?"

"I've been reading about the Amish and everything, and why you remain separate from the world. It's like an escape."

He chuckled. "It's not an escape. It's more like a commitment and also a way of life, committing your life to God and keeping separate from whatever is in the world that can pull you away from God. Well, now I see what you mean by an escape. Maybe it is, in a way."

"Anyway, is there a way that I could do... I don't know, like a trial run?"

His mouth fell open and he stared at her. "Are you serious?"

"I am serious. Don't they do trial runs?"

"Before someone can join us, the bishop usually suggests that the person stays with a family for at least six months to see how they do, so I guess that's a trial run. With us being married already, the bishop might allow you to be with me. Then there are the instructions, which take several weeks, and then there is the baptism where you officially join." He swallowed hard. He was already scheduled to get baptized soon, but he feared telling her that.

"If I came here, I'd have to live with you and your parents?"

They had just reached the cottage, and he stopped the buggy. "How about we live here?"

She looked at where he nodded his head. "It's so sweet. Whose is it?"

"Ours."

She frowned at him. "What do you mean, 'Ours?'"

"It's a miracle, a gift from God and my family, that's what it is. My brothers all pitched in to build it and pay for the materials, and the land belongs to my parents, well, they're going to put paperwork in and officially gift it to me, to us."

She looked at him, and then looked back at the house. "You mean, we have a house?"

"We do now. I've still got a few debts left, but ..."

Tears spilled down her cheeks. "Are you serious? We have a house of our very own?"

He nodded and tried to fight back tears of his own. "That's right. We have a miracle house."

"I thought having our own house would be twenty years or more away for us. I thought it would be when Miranda would be old enough for college, or something."

He wiped the tears away from his eyes and she saw his tears and giggled. He leaned over and tenderly wiped the tears from her cheeks.

"Thank you, Timothy. Things are working out for us already. There is light at the end of a very dark tunnel. I feel we're coming to the end of things."

"No, Taylor. We're at the very beginning." He reached over and hugged Taylor and his baby, and she rested her head on his shoulder. "Wait 'til you see the inside. It's even better." He jumped out of the buggy and hurried around to her side, took Miranda carefully, and helped his wife climb down. Then he passed Miranda back.

When he opened the door for Taylor, he was immediately impressed how beautiful the highly polished floorboards looked, even though he'd seen them before. Mary Lou and his other sisters-in-law had done their best to make it look homey and warm inside. The furniture was lightly used, hand-me-down pieces, and Mary Lou and his mother had made the drapes. Hazel had given him one of the quilts that her mother had made.

"This is so beautiful." She gasped when she walked into the kitchen. "Oh my, and look at the view."

Timothy chuckled at her pleasure. Benjamin had been right; it was a good spot to build a house. Timothy took Miranda out of Taylor's arms. "Go have a look at the bedrooms."

She walked through the house and Timothy followed.

"I can't believe you did all this for me."

"My brothers and my father and I did it, and Mary Lou helped organize them. Benjamin found the land for me. It's the first I've realized how much my family loves me, and now you and Miranda, too."

"I'm so grateful to them all. You know how my parents are. I've never seen anything like this before, done just out of love and with no strings attached."

He so wanted to ask the next question; whether she wanted to talk with the bishop to get things rolling, but wisely held his tongue. He was learning to be less impulsive and more patient.

She turned around to face him, stood on her tiptoes and kissed him, a real kiss. It was awkward to kiss her back while holding the baby, but he managed. "Now," she said, "just how do I go about this trial run?"

"You want to? Really?"

"Yeah."

"You wouldn't be able to finish your studies."

"I know that."

"All you have to do is talk to the bishop, and he'll tell us what needs to be done."

"And you'll come with me?"

"Of course I will." He hoped it would go well. What if she tried it and couldn't cope? He deliberately quieted his fearful thoughts, planning to ask the bishop about delaying his baptism, hoping that he and Taylor might be baptized on the same day. "We have a gas-powered washing machine. *Mamm* and *Dat* gave us their old one and it still works really well."

"Oh, I didn't even think of things like that."

"We won't have electricity, but we can still use most things by battery power or gas."

"Ah." She walked back into the kitchen. "Is that powered by gas?" She pointed to the fridge.

"It is, and it works wonderfully. Would you like a cold drink? Mary Lou said she'd stocked a few basic things."

"Not right now, but thanks." She looked around again. "You've done so much, Timothy, and I foolishly thought you'd forgotten us."

"Never. Not in a million years. All day, every day, no matter what I'm doing, all I think about is you and Miranda." He looked down at the baby in his arms. "I've missed her so much."

"Can you make me an appointment with the bishop?"

He chuckled. "I certainly will."

"I want to move back with you as soon as possible. Are you living here now?"

"Not without you. I want us to be here together, so it's truly both of ours. We'll move here at the same time, depending on what the bishop says. He already knows about you."

She nodded. "I guessed that."

"Do you want to sit out on the porch for a while?"

She nodded and followed him outside.

As she sat down with Timothy, she felt awful that she'd walked out on him, but maybe it was something that had needed to be done so her thinking would change. It had pushed him to make some changes, too. Now, she had a new respect for him and his whole family. They'd gone to a lot of trouble for her and for Timothy. It showed her his family was a true family and she wanted Miranda to be surrounded by that kind of real love—the love that she never got growing up.

TIMOTHY AND TAYLOR sat on the porch chairs, the same ones that used to be on his parents' porch. With his wife by his side and his daughter in his arms, he no longer feared anything. God had brought them this far, so much farther than Timothy could manage in his own strength. It was a miracle that Taylor wanted to join his community, a true miracle, just like this beautiful baby and this house. Now Timothy knew first-hand how good God meant for life to be for his followers. All he had to do was put God first. He would remind himself daily to do just that.

SEVEN AMISH BACHELORS

Book 1 The Amish Bachelor

Book 2 His Amish Romance

Book 3 Joshua's Choice

Book 4 Forbidden Amish Romance

Book 5 The Quiet Amish Bachelor

Book 6 The Determined Amish Bachelor

Book 7 Amish Bachelor's Secret

BOXED SETS

Seven Amish Bachelors Boxed Set Books 1 - 4

Seven Amish Bachelors Boxed Set Books 5-7

ALL BOOK SERIES

Amish Maids Trilogy

Amish Love Blooms

Amish Misfits

The Amish Bonnet Sisters

Amish Women of Pleasant Valley

Ettie Smith Amish Mysteries

Amish Secret Widows' Society

Expectant Amish Widows

Seven Amish Bachelors

Amish Foster Girls

Amish Brides

Amish Romance Secrets

Amish Twin Hearts

Amish Wedding Season

Amish Baby Collection

Gretel Koch Jewel Thief

ABOUT SAMANTHA PRICE

USA Today Bestselling author, Samantha Price, wrote stories from a young age, but it wasn't until later in life that she took up writing full time. Formally an artist, she exchanged her paintbrush for the computer and, many best-selling book series later, has never looked back.

Samantha is happiest on her computer lost in the world of her characters. She is best known for The Amish Bonnet Sisters series and the Expectant Amish Widows series.

www.SamanthaPriceAuthor.com

Samantha loves to hear from her readers. Connect with her at:
www.facebook.com/SamanthaPriceAuthor
Follow Samantha Price on BookBub
Twitter @ AmishRomance
Instagram - SamanthaPriceAuthor
samantha@samanthapriceauthor.com

Made in the USA
Monee, IL
09 March 2022

92589882R10103